Autobiographies of an Angel

GÁBOR SCHEIN

Autobiographies of an Angel

A NOVEL

Translated from the Hungarian by
Ottilie Mulzet

A MARGELLOS
WORLD REPUBLIC OF LETTERS BOOK

Yale UNIVERSITY PRESS | NEW HAVEN & LONDON

English translation copyright © 2022 by Ottilie Mulzet.
Originally published as *Egy angyal önéletrajzai* in 2009 by Jelenkor. This translation is based on a revised version of the original Hungarian text with further structural edits.

Excerpt from an 1877 speech by Alfred Krupp, translated by Edwin Fink and published in 1928 is reprinted by permission, courtesy of *German History in Documents and Images,* German Historical Institute, Washington, D.C.

Yale University Press books may be purchased in quantity for educational, business, or promotional use. For information, please e-mail sales.press@yale.edu (U.S. office) or sales@yaleup.co.uk (U.K. office).

Set in Source Serif type by Motto Publishing Services.
Printed in the United States of America.

Library of Congress Control Number: 2021947404
ISBN 978-0-300-24741-1 (hardcover : alk. paper)

A catalogue record for this book is available from the British Library.

This paper meets the requirements of ANSI/NISO Z39.48-1992 (Permanence of Paper).

10 9 8 7 6 5 4 3 2 1

The Rabbi Jeremiah ben Elazar said: The Holy One,
Blessed be His name, created two faces on the first man,
for surely it is written: You have formed me behind and
before; upon me, You have placed Your hand.

&

as the rings of the traces of two oars
entwine round each other in the water, for a moment
the form of the number eight is clearly seen,
then the ripples become blurred.
perhaps there is a kind of distance from which
endless birth and disappearance
may be precisely observed, if the boats
proceed in one direction, and neither one
is quicker, or slower,
than the other. but do two such boats
in reality exist? infinity is the simultaneous,
accidental beating of two oars, and if there is a pair of eyes
that can read the diagrams of the river,
that too is precisely such a gaze, inadvertently opening.

Contents

Autobiographies of an Angel

Prologue

Somebody has spread the word about me that I understand the Jews. Understand the Jews? Who in the world are they? Do they even exist? It is my belief that Jews don't exist at all; it's not possible to meet up with them, not even in the places where they tend to congregate, such as the synagogues—in the synagogues there are no Jews. The people who are there simply remember something fervently, and they make us remember something. They make us remember that however long our story might be, we do not know— we *still* do not know—what relation connects one person to another, and never shall we know, because history is mythology, a sealed book, a forgotten testimony, an enigma which can never be solved. That is why the single being of history is the Jew, our neighbor who isn't anywhere at all, who, due to some incomprehensible punishment, is forever set apart. The Jew is the wanderer of the twilight of the ages. That is why the Jews cannot be understood. And *I* am the one who would understand them? Madness. The truth is that I understand nothing. At certain times I am sent out, I am born, and I live as best I can and in good spirits.

And it's no wonder that I'm sent out so rarely—that is to say accidentally—at most once every two hundred years, and even then they make sure I don't get mixed up in any important matters, because certainly I would make a mess of them. I have never caused any wars to break out, never made any peace, and invented nothing that might have made my fellow human beings either happier or unhappier. Had I not taken care to ensure a trace remained of my various lives, no one else would do so in my place. No one else would compose a novel or verse about me, and those great charlatans of time, the historians, would never mention me. And yet I can justifiably state that I belong among those noteworthy and rare specimens whom the world has never plundered, truly from the mere fact that I still exist and I do not fall victim at every hour to piratical assaults. While others plunge into the dream of habitude, never forgetting for a moment their goals, I expect nothing and never forget to wonder at the passing of time.

Thus I have lived, since the beginning of the world, many lives in complete insignificance, for the most part in a mirthful humor and with never-ceasing curiosity toward my own self. I have never been able to gain enough of that magnificent endowment by which I can see others and am seen by them, hear others and am heard by them, may touch others and be touched by them; and I always held it to be so splendid that these two things will never be one—my ears, my eyes, and my hands are not self-reflecting mirrors; I am at once the pursuer and the pursued. And yet at times my gaiety clouds over, and for this I blame the simultaneous longevity and brevity of my memories. If I were to remember everything I had ever seen and everything that happened to me, I would have rolled across all my previous lives like a large wine cask, tapped only by bursts of laughter. And it would be the same as if I'd forgotten everything. For is there any more liberated and consequently happier being than he who remains at the beginning, no matter how long he has lived? Nature, though, has endowed me with memory such that no matter how much is poured into me from above, a goodly part of it flows out from below; I have lost much from the joys of the visible world, too much of the sediment of time has turned sour within me, and I come upon its joys all too rarely. This sediment forms my last two lives. As for the rest of them, I know they must be somewhere, although I cannot conjure them up, and yet the story of my wanderings would be complete only with them. Still, I do not regret this, and I do not complain, for surely I, the early pampered being of existence, have been granted the joys of speech— and I have been granted you, my dear reader, whom I do not have to imagine, for you are here in your full reality. You have come from the world into this book, and now it is my hope that you will remain here, that you will be my companion and thus save me from failure. Because—do not forget— it is up to you as well to ensure you find this book worthy and valuable, as if from time to time you were sending me a missive of support, assuring me of your wish yet for this work to be born. If in youth writers passionately pursue their own paths, rejecting others' demands, as they grow old they are immoderately pleased at signs of interest, since nothing else will incite them to new activities. Hoping thus that health and mood will join in alliance, and there will be empty hours for writing, I shall begin to note down my last two lives.

1

Fleeings

I, Johann Klarfeld—once upon a time, I was he—was born as a favored child of the stars on Wednesday, October 13, 1723, in Bittenfeld, next to the town of Waiblingen, precisely at midday, as the church bells began to ring twelve. Venus, in the sign of Libra, began to move closer to the sun, the mutual reception of both Saturn and Jupiter promised auspicious support, only Mars gazed hostilely from beneath Cancer at the divine planet wandering toward Capricorn, while the aspect of Mercury was barely visible in Scorpio. It is certainly these propitious signs I have to thank that I remained alive at all; due to the unskillfulness of the midwife, it appeared that I came into the world as dead, and it was only after not a few exertions were applied that life was breathed back into me. My father, Nicolaus Klarfeld, was arranging his community affairs that day: the younger of my two great-aunts ran to bring him news of my birth. How unfortunate that I myself could not perform that task.

Our house, an old building of two stories, stood in the vicinity of the Ulrichkirche, and was hedged round, in that tiny Swabian nest (itself having been depopulated many times over by the plague) with respectability: rumors and doubtful jokes could not penetrate it. My parents lived with my younger sisters on the lower floor, which opened on to a spacious veranda. We children loved most to spend time there. The veranda was closed off from the street by a large wooden lattice. Such birdcages, which were appended to many houses, were known as frames. Here the women would sit, here they would do their sewing and their knitting, here is where the cook would pick the lettuce, and it was from here that the women neighbors would call out to each other, which in the warmer months lent the street the appearance of a locale in the southern climes. People were at ease, well acquainted with public existence.

My mother's two older sisters, who lived on the second floor, took care, however, to ensure that our lives were not so fully free and easy, and that we too might know the premonition of fear. A tower-like flight of stairs led up to their rooms, a flight of stairs that seemed endless to me, although it could not have been constructed of more than fifteen or at most sixteen steps. These two disconsolate spinsters knew, better than anyone, the rules of a proper and desirable life, ceaselessly furnishing not only us children with their well-intentioned guidance but our mother and father as well. I did not wonder at the mildness with which our mother received these counsels, but my father's resistance I found to be insufficiently energetic; thus it became my conviction that as far as our upbringing was concerned these two great-aunts would one day take full command, and if this turn of events did not completely come to pass just as I had pictured it, I was nonetheless certain: that day would be the most bitter of my entire life hitherto.

My father insisted—even without the advice of the two aunts—that my education commence at an early age. Thus at seven years old I could already write properly, and do some counting as well. At the urging of my private tutor, I also attempted to study some Latin, and although I found the grammar to be nothing more than an aggregate of arbitrary legalities with a certain amount of rote memorization—my propensity for it necessarily aided by frequent blows and the threatening swish of the cane—before long I could say about myself that the arts of declination and conjugation were no longer foreign to me. When I think about those years today and I try to evoke the face of my father, whom my increasing knowledge surely must have made happy, seeking to recall his features as he drilled me in the conjugations of the verbs *discludo* and *concurso,* the painting of memory remains blank.

Yet memory and imagination spring from one root: they are twins who often slip into identical garments, finding much pleasure in this play. Namely, they grant features to no one; they take the countenance away but never run out of stories. Accordingly, I myself can hardly begin to guess which one of them is responsible for what I recall of Nicolaus Klarfeld, and I do not investigate whether it is true or not, although I somehow believe—given the equal insistence of both imagination and memory—that it must be true, albeit the knowledge I derive from these stories is not exactly pleasant.

My father's parents were Jews, and he himself resembled those little boys with their earlocks whom I used to see and hear in Böblingen as, jabbering incomprehensibly, they teemed in the narrow and filthy Jewish street situated between the city wall and the moat. Their cacophonous language—the living memory of a dark and primitive age—always exercised the most unpleasant of effects upon me whenever I had to pass in front of the Jewish gate, casting but a mere glance inside. What would have happened if the upstanding burghers of Bittenfeld were to suspect that my father belonged to that misshapen and jostling people, who never run short of excessive demands and offers? For if I may believe memory and its hallucinations, this is surely the truth. My father spent his childhood in the North, in Hannover, his father—for this much notability I cannot deny him, especially as in doing so I also grant it to myself—was a merchant, but of course only a minor one; he was not one of those traders who traveled to faraway lands, not one of those who went to Amsterdam and beyond, sending their wagons for export, loaded with fabrics, ivy, and silver, as had the unsuspecting Job at one time.

It is a well-known fact that in the autumn the Jews celebrate their High Holy Days. If previously they had traveled far, either by foot or by horse cart, then at this time they came home, because this was the law, the entire day barely sticking their noses outside their temples; with their bowing and chanting they tried to win back the favor of that God of whom their writings speak. Once it happened that in the morning of such a festive day, when his mother began to dress my father (whom I imagine being as old as I was at the time of his death), or, strictly speaking, that boy whom, in my lifetime, I had to regard as my father, he winced in pain. His mother asked what the problem was. My father raised his arm: beneath it was a good-sized scarlet abscess, uniform. His mother didn't panic; she knew what to do. She instructed the servant girl to go to the synagogue, ask my father's father for the barber's address, come back, and take the boy there for a plaster. She enjoined her to utter not one word if anyone began badgering her about the urgent need for the barber.

The servant girl had to pass through the women's section before she could get to the men. When she came back, an old Polish beggar woman spoke to her, asking her what business she had there. As the beggar woman was a stranger in Hannover, the servant girl did not think that my grandmother's warning applied to the old Polish woman, and she must have felt relieved about having completed her mission in the men's section of the synagogue, so she betrayed my father's illness. The women sitting nearby overheard and grew terrified. The Polish beggar woman said she understood every kind of abscess—for twenty years she had met up with more than enough of such cases—and she herself would go and take a look at the boy. The servant girl accompanied the beggar woman, and when she saw the abscess, she immediately raised a hue and cry, yelling, "Flee, flee, the plague is in your house!" At the sound of the yelling, many ran out of the synagogue, and my father, along with the servant girl, was driven with long canes out into the street. Every thrust of the canes hurt him. The people of Hannover knew that the plague was spread by pork. His mother wailed that there was nothing wrong with her son: he ate no pork at all, he had not eaten a single piece of pork, he didn't even know its smell. The plague, however, which could only be caused by pork, was present, and the Jews were afraid that if news of the illness reached the prince, everything they owned would be burned and they themselves would be driven out from the vicinity. The men therefore decided that the servant girl and my father together had to go in rags and torn clothes to a nearby village, to knock on a peasant's door and say that the Jews of Hannover had not given them lodging during the High Holidays, for they had already put up many poor people, but they promised to send abundant food and drink to the village if they were given shelter. They sent the Polish beggar woman with them, and in view of the danger (and to help keep her quiet), they gave her thirty thalers. In one house they were received by upright people. The Jews of Hannover amassed a great quantity of food, but they did not allow my father's father to take it alone into the village. His brother-in-law went with him. When they saw my father at the edge of the village, my grandfather wanted to run over to him, but his brother-in-law grabbed his arm. They placed the bundle at the edge of the field, stepped back, and let the beggar woman go in his place. My grandfather saw that the boy was healthy, but there was nothing he could do. Eight days passed in this way. The beggar woman had plasters and ointments, everything needed to treat an abscess; by the eighth day not even a trace remained. My grandfather asked the Jews of Hannover how long they planned to insist on these idiocies—they knew quite well that his son, Saul, was healthy, so they should let him back into the city. Of course, I cannot know what my father's name was at that time; it might have been Solomon or it might have been Isaac—as far as I'm concerned it could have been Abraham too, and yet I name him Saul not only because Saul was the first king of Israel who chased all those with familiar spirits and wizards out of the land, but also because this was the name of the great wanderer of Damascus. Therefore I believe that no other name is as suitable for my father, although in his case the world, which for him was no larger than Bittenfeld and its surroundings, will honor his good name as Nicolaus. Accordingly, when my grandfather said that his son, Saul, was healthy, once again the men gathered, and they pondered and pondered until they finally agreed there was no problem with the boy—they themselves had ascertained it; after eight days he could return. There was nothing else to do but to wait out his time. When the second period of eight days had come to an end, and my father was allowed to return, everyone wept: my grandfather, my grandmother, and my father's siblings. They all thought they were crying for joy. They were not, however, crying for joy: they were crying because they were bidding farewell to my father, who had not been with them in the synagogue when the Angel of Life wrote their names in the great white book. True, he had not been there either when shortly afterward the bespectacled Angel of Death had walked through the aisles, adding a new name here or there to the list of names it noted down in the fine black leatherbound book, as if this were the finest of jokes causing every person of good taste to burst out laughing. Specifically, the Jews believe that during their autumn Holy Days it is decided whose time has come to an end, even if that person feels stronger than ever before and never so full of plans as in that moment when he must give up his soul. It has been decided, and the decision must be fulfilled. My father's name, however, was inscribed in neither the white nor the black book; neither the Angel of Life nor the Angel of Death knew about him. For it is well known that they both conduct their bookkeeping in the fashion of an eyeglass merchant, subtracting the mortalities of this year from the previous year's balance carried forward, then factoring in the increase; and as my father no longer figured in either of their account books, his name was erased from the register of the names of the Jews. After this he lived three more years in his parents' house, then he ran away. How he did this I do not know. He cut off his earlocks, he converted to the honorable faith of the Lutherans, and when he was baptized he chose for himself the name Nicolaus, in which of course his old name was concealed. Now there was no longer any angel that could ever come upon him. He became a fervent Lutheran, his voice resounding in the church chorus so heartrendingly as he sang "Gott, warum verstößest du uns für immer und bist so zornig über die Schafe deiner Weide?" No one could ever have suspected that the upstanding Nicolaus might, at times in secret, perhaps be thinking of another flock of gentle lambs: the one he had left behind.

My father took this secret with him to the grave. He was no longer a Jew. But just as no one can ever be wholly certain that he is not a Jew, that he has completely succeeded in absolutely not being that, so it is that secrets never fully disappear: there is never a thick enough layer of earth or sky to shovel on top of them; there will always remain some trace, just enough for a story to emerge from them again one day. The secret awaits, biding its time, then appearing at the most unexpected moment, and as is true of secrets that crop up unexpectedly, my father's secret also desired blood, and blood was almost spilled, and it is truly only thanks to good luck and the goodwill of a few people that nothing fatal occurred.

After that was a time of waiting nearly two centuries long. In my last life hitherto, I was born on December 6, 1944, in a tiny northeastern village in Hungary, in Csokvaomány, appropriately on the name day of Saint Nicholas, in memory of the deceased Nicolaus Klarfeld. If on that day my father,

Nándor Józsa, had been at home, and my grandparents at lunch had asked him how the girl child looked, he certainly would have answered that I looked like an ugly little piglet, because even then I was decidedly no beauty, but he would have laughed, and my grandparents would have laughed at this too. But he wasn't home, because just then he was digging anti-tank ditches in Germany; he said nothing at lunch, and perhaps there wasn't even any lunch that day, but I, certainly, was born: Ye have heard, unto the Józsa family a little piglet was born.

I got my name—in this life I was called Berta—after one of my grandmothers, but according to the village gossip I was named after the cannon known by the same name during the First World War, Big Bertha, because I too was bulky, and as it turned out later on, I was stubborn Berta as well, just like a boy, they said: the poor thing takes after her father. And my mother sent me out as if I were a boy. She cut my hair short, completely short, saying that at least this way I wouldn't get lice. Although I got lice all the same. The tiny insects moved around on my head, living off my blood. My mother tied a vinegar-soaked kerchief on my head, and now beneath the kerchief I was completely bald, and my hair grew out again only very slowly. And yet the baldness was somehow connected, or at least I thought so, to the fact that in the village everyone started to call me little Jewish girl. Come here, little Jewish girl. Maybe it wasn't even then that they started to call me that, maybe I'd only started noticing it. I had heard about how the Germans had shaved the heads of the Jewish women, and I could picture all the bald women. I thought that was the reason why. And I could not forgive my mother for shaving my head. It was around that time I noticed that if

I messed something up, or if I didn't do something I should have, my mother would say that the good God should put me in with the bald ones. I couldn't even imagine what this meant.

But there's plenty of time for me to tell you about that little bald Jewish girl. I can start now though, because that waiting time of two hundred years took no longer for me than the time it will take for you to read one page of this book; everything happened almost simultaneously: my father's escape, my escape, the endless enumeration of our sins and crimes. The days of the Angels, like the days of people, are like blades of grass. If the wind passes through them they are no more, and nothing will ever remind us of their place. But you see I'm still here; you're listening to me, and I'm talking to you. I live in that ruinous interstice caused by the slippage of times, of which most people know only the two shores: yesterday and today, life and death; in vain are they without possessions on this earth. I, however, recognize neither one. I know neither the past nor the future. Everything is now; life is in love with death, it yearns for it impotently.

Time does not pass, it merely comes to ruin, and in the midst of this ruin no one knows where he stands. Still, though, we must use the accustomed designations of time. In the autumn of 1733, in one or another of these hours of his ruin, my father, Nicolaus Klarfeld, fell to his bed, his fever soared, and despite careful nursing, medicaments, and cooling compresses, he quickly died. He left my mother alone with a middling property and eight children. A bitter life began for me then; I do not speak of its wretchedness gladly. The house which stood in the vicinity of the Ulrich-kirche against which many loans had been taken was sold by my mother, and in its place she bought a dwelling on a good-sized piece of land located on the edge of the city. The aunts came there with us too: they could not have done otherwise, as my mother's younger brother, resident in Ulm, would not take them in. This new life into which we were plunged, so to speak, with no preparation at all, came with much unpleasantness, and we could not count upon any assistance. My poor mother suffered ignoble things from her relatives and acquaintances. We children, however, who until then had been kept apart, tidy, noble, and under strict supervision, regretted our lost life, although we also rejoiced at our newly gained freedom, and neither was the grime—impossible to keep out of the house—our adversary.

In the first weeks after we had moved in, stonemasons and carpenters were still working in every corner of the house because my mother had bought it in a half-decrepit state, and it was wise of her to do so, for she could reconstruct it according to her own wishes. She turned her greatest concern to the placement of the plate-glass windows, so the rooms would be completely filled with light: in our previous house, which faced north, the windows had been small, and thus we had to do without. My mother supervised the work of renovation; the stonemasons and the carpenters, however, were noisy as they strolled around—as if they were in their own home, they behaved in an arrogant and swaggering manner toward my mother, reassuring her that they were striving for the very best outcome in everything, and although it seemed they truly did know their trade, I had the impression that among themselves they laughed at her and cheated her if they could. I of course admired them: I admired their tools as well, the pickaxes, the ladles, the hatchets, and most of all the clever windlass mechanism. I could spend all day watching the scaffolding being erected, the leisurely rhythm of construction; but in the evening, when they left, my younger sisters and I happily swung on the planks that were left sticking out.

I recall that in these weeks I saw hardly a trace of the two aunts. When everything had been put in order they returned and once again took over command of the household. They ordered us all out to the fields, and although I greatly doubt their hands had ever known the blister made by the hoe, they decided, brooking no dissent, what we would plant and where, perpetually admonishing us children that we must help our poor mother lest she be killed by all the work, you don't even know what a good mother you have. Veritably, they were in their element. We planted lettuce, peas, beans, potatoes, squash, kohlrabi, and rhubarb, so we could take all the produce to the Böblingen market. Of course from this it was not possible to live sumptuously. That is why my mother, who earlier had played very beautifully on the virginal but who since my father's illness had not once lifted its lid, now once again began to play, and she went to a few of the burghers in the city in order to teach music to their children, because at that time private music tutoring had come into fashion even among households of lesser means. But there was no more money for me to continue my studies. Following our aunts' command, my younger sisters and I worked the land—they considered this an excellent method of upbringing, being of the opinion that digging with the shovel, beating away clumps of soil, tying up bunches of vegetables, and eternally ripping weeds out of the earth worked wonders for a child's character. And as I was now the only man of the house, as they put it, the hardest work always fell to me, even though in matters of physical strength I was not any more developed than my sisters. There was, however, some recompense for the exhausting work in its end result. I liked the market square when the sellers took it over, as well as the strange figures who appeared everywhere on their heels: the showmen, the bakers with their milk loaves, the fortune-tellers, the tricksters. I happily counted the money we earned from our produce, especially since I could always pinch a few groschen, which we then used to buy sheets of printed paper stamped with animal figures, but whenever I thought of the next day's work, the bile would rise in my throat: I would have been more than happy to scrape my poor father out of the earth.

After a while I began to entreat my mother to let me go. Specifically I had taken it into my head that somehow I would once again continue what I had been deprived of after my father's death, namely, my studies. My mother soon realized that I felt no pangs of conscience whatsoever at the idea of depriving the family of a pair of working hands; in vain did she paint their future without me in dark hues. What would happen? My younger sisters would soon marry, bringing men into the house, upstanding boys, and with this the retreat would finally sound for the aunts. My pleas finally attained their goal, my mother's heart relented, and to my greatest amazement, this time she even stood up for me against the aunts, who called me ungrateful. Thus in the spring of 1738 I left Bittenfeld, never to see my mother again. I made my way to Denkendorf, where I went into apprenticeship with Master Fröschlin, whose greatest wish was to become the barber for the local monastery.

2

With Weary Eyes, Blinking

As my previous life had consisted of continuous wandering, and as I can say I never longed to return to that place from which I had once come, my last life became one of attachment. And yet it was not I who was attached; instead it was a village that became attached to me. Its streets, on which no one ever seemed to be heading outward, only backward, even when dead, coiled around me like clumps of seaweed. The stories were always the stories of those who had returned, the stories of actual men and women who wanted not only to hope and to remember but to live as well. Yet whoever wants to live would do well first to traverse the world, and if a choice must be made between birth and death, he should begin with death. In this way he will not be deceived by ruinous time, nor will his soul become too mired in comfort: he will not follow the false plans of hope, judge his own self, or allow himself to pay for his own wretchedness with the last farthings of memory.

A beginning is always a repetition, although we should not necessarily believe that that which returns has ended up in a good place; yet the fact that one has a place at all in this world means that one is, therefore, alive—and what else could be the cause of that, if not repetition? This is what my grandfather could have thought as well, when in 1916 or 1917 he received a gunshot wound to the stomach somewhere in Galicia. He lay on the wide, snow-covered field, his stomach split open, and the sun, looming through the squalor of the November sky, looked down into him. And there were two other pairs of eyes looking into him: they belonged to two men from the village and were the eyes of two brothers, because my grandfather had marched in with these men and they would never abandon each other. Now, though, his time had come. My grandfather lay there beneath the November sky, and while the men did not make it home until the following spring their first port of call was to my grandmother, to bring her the news that they'd seen my grandfather perish in Galicia. He had received a gunshot wound to the stomach and had not lived to see the morning.

And so my grandmother did what one must at such times. She had mass said for him, she had the church bells rung, and she lamented. The weeks and the months went by, the first winter passed, then the second, and then, at the beginning of March, when, on the forest paths above, the water beneath the ice on the frozen puddles had begun to move, her husband came home. He himself had no idea how long he had been lying half-dead in the snow. Time had stopped, but his eyes were open. He said, "You don't even know what snow is, you don't even know what cold is." A peasant found him underneath the November sky. He had come to remove whatever items the dead bodies still had on them. He turned out the pockets of the dead men, he yanked off their coats, their combat jackets, he pulled off their boots; the broken leather, frozen hard, could still be used for something. And when he heard one of them still moaning, he went over, and he saw what a beautiful strapping man this was; he didn't strike him dead but managed to get him into his ramshackle buggy, took him home, and got him back to health within a few weeks. My grandfather worked for this man: he turned the earth over for him—he was grateful to him for his life, but not so much that he didn't run away at the end of the summer. My grandfather came home by foot all the way from Galicia. At the border he met up with a troop of prisoners of war. A train was taking them back to Miskolc. At the station, gendarmes were waiting for them. They asked each man if he knew Russian. Anyone who answered no was arrested as a deserter. The ones who decided they knew Russian were ordered back into the freight car, and since they must have absorbed Bolshevism along with the Russian tongue, were deported straight back to Russia. My grandfather, however, was telling the truth: he had learned some Russian when he was with the peasant—that is, he had picked up some Ukrainian, which was almost the same thing. Even as an old man he still remembered a few words. When the gendarme ordered him back into the freight car and he realized what it meant, my grandfather pushed aside the bayonet-wielding gendarme, for he preferred to die there than go back. "You go back yourself!" he yelled. At least this is how he told the story, and as for me, as I write it down I have no objection to the idea that once in his life he might have felt brave, that anyone hearing this story might imagine him as brave—brave, terrified, or exhausted to the point of insanity: in front of a gendarme's bayonet, it's all one. He shoved aside the gendarme, and before he or the other gendarmes could react, my grandfather disappeared into the crowd. He didn't dare go back into the village, fearing they would search for him. Needless to say, no one did. When the Czechoslovak army marched into northern Hungary, he went home. This was dictated by his sense of rhythm. He went home gladly, because he had already seen quite enough of the world outside. The dead man came home. There in front of my grandmother stood that strapping man. Neither of them knew what they were supposed to say when someone comes back from the dead.

The Czechoslovaks soon left, and in their place came the Romanians. They rounded up all the men into the schoolhouse and gave them a thorough beating. This, of course, is always the prerogative of an occupying army, if only so that it will be remembered. My grandfather became a caustic, hard man. He was often ill, an invalid, as they used to say, the kind of person needed by no one. He worked with the maintenance crew in the mine. He couldn't go underground because his lung had also been pierced at the front. He brought home the newspapers from the mining office, *Népszava,* the *People's Voice,* but never the *Kis Újság,* the *Little Newspaper,* or *Pest Diary,* because he supported the Social Democratic Party, although I don't know exactly what this meant in his case. He didn't get too involved in organizing the strikes. Maybe he only found out what "social democrat" meant when he was beaten up again in 1948, this time because his sense of rhythm had dictated that he did not wish to switch allegiance and sign up with the Communist Party. From that point on he never read any newspapers in the evening, not even the *People's Voice.* My grandmother would place a mug of sour buttermilk on the table in front of him just as she had done every evening since he had come home from the dead, and slurping his buttermilk, his gaze fixed on a faraway and fraying memory of a snow-covered field, he disappeared from the family memory. After him there remained in the house eternal snow, dying, and frost. Only something about which there was nothing to say. And of course there was no reason to be silent. There simply were no words with which anything could have been said.

And no such words were produced later either. Twenty years passed; the cold remained. It was as if there were eternal winter beneath the Bükk Mountains; the snow kept falling. And not only was birth repeated, so was death. War broke out again, and Nándor Józsa, who in this life was my father, was called up. After being sent to both Újvidék and Ruthenia, he was taken to Russia, where he too was injured. He had withdrawn with his troop into a bunker on the banks of the Dnieper, and they were almost out of ammunition when the Russians fired a grenade into it. All the men around him were killed immediately. His own face was suffused with a pleasant languor; he felt no pain. He fell out of time: he didn't know how many minutes, how many hours, how many days had gone by. He felt joy, a slow, measured joy, if there is such a thing: the summer evening sky stretched over him like a soft blanket. The sun was already going down. When he came to himself, he was lying outside in front of the bunker, and one of the men from his troop, a Rom, who it seemed had also escaped the explosion with minor wounds, was yanking at his combat jacket for him to wake up, the Russians would be here any minute now. But my father couldn't stand up, and he didn't see how they could find a better place than this to die. He didn't try to help the Rom, who then had to lift him; he began dragging him through the mud toward the hill. Just as in one of those Soviet partisan movies. At least that's how he told the story.

But the body of a helpless man is unbearably heavy. Heavier than mud. Still, the Rom dragged him along, and what was awaiting them at the top of the hill did not so much resemble a Soviet partisan movie as a Swiss postcard. Two cows, tethered to a tree, grazed peacefully. They weren't fat cows, but they weren't scrawny, either. For them there was no war. They munched on the grass. In other words, thought my father, this would be the place, and although it wasn't completely according to his taste, he consented to the Rom's choice: he was going to die in the middle of a Swiss postcard. It was no fault of theirs it didn't happen like that. Before they managed to reach the rectangular field of the postcard and were only a stone's throw from the top of the hill, another grenade exploded, this time right between the cows, and like some kind of mirage the Swiss postcard was torn to shreds, and they were filled with shrapnel. As to what happened after this, neither of them could recall. Somehow they ended up in a Hungarian field hospital, from which my father was transported home by airplane. Not only his body but his eyes were filled with minute sparkling shards, sharp stars like tiny specks. His eyeballs were temporarily removed for the operation. From that point on he could not see well, and one year before his death, he suffered a cerebrovascular spasm: lying in the hospital, he looked up at the sharp light, began to lash at his own body, and fell, trembling, into an epileptic fit.

And yet the stars were never truly faithless to him. Days after his eye operation, the regent himself, Miklós Horthy de Nagybánya, visited him in the Miskolc hospital. Clearly, the regent was still wearing his rear admiral's uniform, which he hadn't taken off since November 16, 1919, when he had

ridden into Budapest on horseback at the head of his officers, slowly proceeding along Fehérvári Road, later named
after him, finally arriving at the recently constructed Seces-
sionist hotel, built on the location of the one-time Virgins'
Baths, where thirty thousand citizens of both Buda and Pest
awaited him in complete certainty as to what would now follow. "Here on the banks of the Danube, I call upon the Hungarian capital city to admit its guilt," Horthy roared above
their heads, "for this city has denied its millennial past, this
city has trampled down and thrown its national colors into
the mud; it has dressed itself in the red rags of Bolshevism.
The city has thrown its finest into prison, driven them out of
the nation, and in one year it has plundered all that was our
best. But the closer we came to it, the more the ice melted
away from our hearts, and we are ready now to forgive." That
is how the rear admiral spoke, in the royal first-person plural; and from the other side of the Danube grateful sighs of
relief ascended, because what might have happened here—
if, in the November cold, the ice hadn't melted away from
Horthy's heart, if it had stayed there, and instead of this
sensitive-souled soldier, an unfeeling ice king had moved
into the Buda Palace—was terrifying even to imagine. But
the ice did melt, and by the time the admiral without a navy
sought out the wounded in 1943 in Miskolc, not only had the
ice melted away from his heart, but the first-person plural
had worn off his tongue. He went alone from one sick ward
to the other, even though he had come with a retinue, and
everything around him was completely white. The light was
white, the face of the deaconess was white, the bandages on
my father's eyes were white as well. And Horthy went over
to every one of the wounded, he went over to the ones who

could still stand, just as he walked over to the ones who would never be able to stand again, he went over to all of them in his ocean-scented admiral's uniform and pinned a silver metal on each of their chests. My father got one too. In his old age he would take it out, looking at it as if he were seeing it for the first time; he would turn it around in his hands, but he did not see the white face of Horthy in that medal, nor did he recall if the regent had said something to him. At least something to the effect of, Get better, my son. Something like, Before too long you will see, you will see the sky again. Or something like, I forgive you. No, my father could not recall a single word. The admiral was plunged into gloomy thought, mutely he went on, and behind him the sick wards grew dark and empty, and in their echoing emptiness railcars clattered, orders were barked out, bombs whistled past, and when my father regained his vision he looked out the window with weary eyes, blinking; he was not sent immediately back to the front but instead was placed with the rank-and-file reserves; he became a policeman in Ózd.

And finally he could see his daughter—that is to say, me. I was an ugly little piglet, scrawny too, what else could I have been at a time like that? Because the times were ugly, they were relentlessly gray and black, but even in such ugly times there are days, or at least hours, which seem to have been conceived under a different, brighter sky; only much, much later did it emerge that even time itself could never have been born from a blacker womb.

It was a day just like that when my father came home with some yarn for knitting a sweater. Where did you get that yarn, Nándor? my mother could have asked, but she didn't because it was such a wonderfully beautiful red yarn, with a white snowflake pattern, that it took her breath away. As if it had been sprinkled with snowflakes. Before too long, a sweater, good and warm, was made from this yarn. Snow fell, but in this pullover, you never felt the cold. And although the times didn't get even a tiny speck brighter—in fact, if it was possible they grew even bleaker—as long as my mother wore the white snowflake-patterned pullover, the breath was trapped in her throat, and not one word came out of my mother, although she certainly would have had something to talk about.

Specifically, in Ózd, on April 17, 1944, the gendarmes rounded up all the Jews from the surrounding villages and dispatched the entire kith and kin to Miskolc, from where in the following months more than fifty thousand people were deported. On the next day, April 18, four or five men, rounded up from the tavern and supervised by the village police, piled everything taken from the Jews onto freight cars—coats, bedlinens, shoes, children's toys—all the things they wouldn't need in the place they were headed. After the wagons were sealed, three policeman remained at the station—they had weapons, but no ammunition. One of them was my father.

At around nine o'clock in the evening, people began to gather around the tracks. What did they want? They'd heard that two freight cars were filled to the brim with fine Jewish possessions. Damask bed linens, lace, wholesale quantities of linen, porcelain, even silver. For a long time the people standing around the tracks didn't move. They began to charge the railcars at about eleven p.m. The entire affair was a hectic pantomime. The policemen stood to one side. These two freight cars weren't worth spilling any blood over. Wretched bedclothes, shirts, and dressing gowns were ripped away out of the darkness. So this is what your women wore! There were jackets, worn-out shoes, children's coats, boy's trousers. Now you know—your houses are not untouchable! Two or three men jumped into the freight cars, and within a minute tossed out the rest of what was inside. Anyone who wanted to get something good had to be sharp-eyed, quick. The whole thing lasted maybe ten minutes. The freight cars were immediately emptied, and on the gravel-covered tracks, in between the rail ties, perhaps only a single hat or one of a pair of shoes remained. In the darkness, they were like the corpses of a fallen animal.

My father watched the entire assault standing next to one of the freight cars. He had known for hours this was going to happen; there was no curiosity within him at all. Let them take whatever they want. The policemen could not be held responsible for this. In the moments after the freight cars had been broken into, a small bundle tied up with string fell onto the ground; in the midst of the people charging toward the railroad cars, somebody had kicked it beneath the wheels. Only a corner of the bundle stuck out, and in the darkness even that couldn't be seen. After all the others had left the station, my father knelt down: he took the bundle out from beneath the wheel. There was quite a lot of yarn in it. Red yarn, with a white snowflake pattern. My father tucked it beneath his jacket, and he brought it home to my mother so she could knit something for herself. My mother had never seen such exquisite yarn. She knitted a sweater using the yarn, which she only wore on holidays. The sweater always had a pure scent of lily of the valley. I would snuggle into it, and, eyes closed, breathe in as much of the lily of the valley fragrance as I could. I didn't know that this fragrance was not my mother's. But then whose was it? Whose fragrance was this, and whose was this eternal snowfall? My father told us the story about the ransacking of the freight cars only ten years later. My mother wept. And I was certain that this yarn belonged to a little girl, a little girl who at that time when another freight car took her away had been four years old, just like me. Someone had been planning to knit her a vest and sweater from that yarn. Only when my father told the story of the yarn, I was the one who was wearing the sweater that had been made from it. My mother had unraveled hers, because the snowflake pattern didn't suit her anymore, and she reknitted it for me. I wore the pullover when spring was coming, and I wore it when I began middle school in September, in Miskolc. By that time, its fragrance of lily of the valley had fled. But the polka dots were still very beautiful, and the snow kept falling heavily. And when my own little girl was ten years old, I too took out a small pair of scissors, cut out the last stitch, and unraveled the yarn of the sweater which I had kept until then. It became a large skein. And as I pulled on each loop, twisting it around my index finger, the stitches sliding across from one needle to the next, I wondered again: How could my father have picked up that bundle from beneath the freight car wheel, how could it have been precisely he who took that bundle, how could he have brought it home to my mother, and why did he allow me to go around in a sweater knitted from that yarn after my mother had done so? How could he have given my mother the death of that little girl? And why did he allow my mother to give it to me? Why didn't my mother take it away from me? For surely she knew by then. She knew everything. Is it possible that she hadn't thought about this at all? The freight car pulled out from the station at Ózd, taking with it the face of that little girl, never seen. The snow fell, it fell and fell. And when I had unraveled the last stitch from that sweater, I was able to cry for the first time in a long while for my father and my mother. And from that yarn, I knitted a cardigan for my daughter. She wore it for a long time, then finally with her the material gave out. And now I want nothing more than to take the end of that frayed yarn into my hands, to once again knit my mother's sweater as well as my own—to once again knit together the falling snow, my own story.

The end of the thread, however—assuming anything that happens in the world has a beginning and an end and that it is not a pair of scissors that places stories into the hands of human beings, or rather a sword, because even the simplest of stories is no simpler than the oxcart's Gordian knot—is not here before me to take up. Instead I must pull it from a tangled skein, and I cannot be sure of reaching for the right thread. Who has eyes for something like that? Namely, my father—who, just a moment ago we observed standing next to the ransacked freight cars, kneeling down and picking up a small bundle tied with string, who before he stood up looked around and concealed that bundle beneath his coat—my father was considered to be a Jew by everyone in the village. Compared to them, he was Jewish. Or at least a little more Jewish than they were.

A long time ago, before he arrived in the village—how beautiful this familial closeness, how beautiful your tent, Jacob, the something of someone, the nothing of no one—my grandfather's mother worked for the pharmacist in Putnok. She washed and cooked for him, and after a while she even helped with the preparation of medicines. Only the pharmacist's name, Salamon Widder, remains. If we are to cautiously fill out this name with the pieces of life that belonged to it, just like an archaeologist beneath the lamp light completing the fragments of jewels and coins through a magnifying glass, we can see a grumbling, unsociable man in the darkness of the pharmacy as he pounds a piece of talcum into powder in a reddish-brown agate mortar: he takes a tiny mound of it on the end of a silver spoon and tips it into a porcelain jar on the pharmaceutical scales. During this operation he never turns toward us so that we might observe him more closely, and when the small bell hung above the door grows silent, and our unanswered greeting dissipates in the air, we, after a brief pause, clear our throats.

The pharmacist's closest friend was Rabbi Lipót Braun. They visited each other frequently, often going for strolls along the streets lined with dark sumac. As to what they discussed while walking around the Serényi Manor House, which had been reconstructed by Count László Serényi only ten years earlier, or on the days when it was raining and the gentlemen retired to the pharmacist's house, no one could guess. Neither could my great-grandmother, who at such times was allowed into the dimly lit library only long enough to carry in a tray piled high with walnut pastries, as this was well known to be the rabbi's favorite; she set down the porcelain cups on the small carpet-covered table because the pharmacist liked to soothe his throat against a chill with elderberry tea, especially with fresh honey stirred in.

As to what these two distinguished gentlemen spoke of, and what was the marrow of their conversations, no one in this barren city of sumac-lined streets could ever surmise, as into their words they mixed with great pleasure all sorts of languages—and yet still we may picture it: sentences containing Talmudic lines about the Tower of Babel, languages, and Adam and his sons rose from one side of the table above the steaming tea, whereas from the other side enigmatic details concerning pharmacology, anatomy, and surgical history sought a path among the carpet's refined arabesques. If this carpet, which on Holy Days migrated to the synagogue to serve as a cover for the Torah reading table, still existed today; if after the pharmacist's death it had not turned up in Sátoraljaújhely as a bequest to Eleázár Lőw who was then called to Ungvár as chief rabbi; then if, on a rainy November day, it had not been placed on a jolting handcart, covered with a peddler's canvas, and taken to the village of Sáta, where, forgotten and battered, it languished in an attic; and if it had not, in this battered state, vanished, as, in full view of my father, the two freight cars were plundered—then we could press our ears to Salamon Widder's carpet and perhaps hear something of those old conversations. Although it is to be feared that even then we would hear nothing more than Lipót Braun's heartrending stuttering, for the rabbi was one of the most hopeless stutterers this earth ever carried on its back—that is, until he stepped up to the lectern, because there it was suddenly as if the angels were moving his tongue: his stuttering vanished, and he pronounced his address without impediment, rocking his body slowly back and forth, frequently closing his eyes as well. But just as that carpet definitively vanished, along with the tea set and its leaf pattern, the pharmacy's entire furnishings, the porcelain jars and their inscriptions, the agate mortar and pharmaceutical scales, neither imagination nor memory can aid either Salamon Widder or Lipót Braun in taking one of their customary strolls around the Serényi Manor House as they examine in detail the reconstruction of the northern wing's Ionic columns. Thus, neither can we glimpse the events of that day when Lipót Braun held his scandalous Rosh Hasha-nah address in the synagogue, the day after which he fell into a high fever and died. That day was September 12, 1872. If we cannot see Lipót Braun as he walks along Tompa Mi-hály Street—back then known as Nameless Street—in his long blue overcoat and his beautiful hat worth a treasure in itself, carrying his walking cane, muttering, and pronounc-ing something like a greeting to the people passing him from the other direction, if we close our eyes tightly, and if we rock our bodies gently back and forth, we may yet hear his address, and the grumbling and the loud hissing of those present shall hardly trouble us.

Lipót Braun did not share the hopes of those who trusted in the rapid acceptance of the Jews; moreover, he did not ap-prove of this great mutual embrace of Jew and Hungarian, and yet he had been for twenty years already one of the first rabbis to regularly deliver his sermons in Hungarian. Now, however, he cautioned those present that that language which the Jews of Putnok had voluntarily renounced was the same one from which they had drawn their strength so as to pronounce holy things within it. He particularly emphasized the word *holy,* nearly spitting it out of his mouth as if he had bitten a pepper seed in two: certainly his nostrils trembled, and his left eyebrow, positioned higher on his face, rose in an even more pronounced arc. So it was not possible to know if the thought that holiness was mute—moreover, the name of God was lost—filled him with wise resignation or, on the contrary, if his words were a reflection of the acrimonious maliciousness so characteristic of polyglots.

Lipót Braun paused at length after the first sentence; closing his eyes, he became immersed in his own self, then suddenly he grew enlivened, and continued, "When God created the heavens, the earth, and the living beings of the earth, and He entrusted people to name the animals that live upon the earth, above the earth, and in the waters, He forgot about two things. He did not give names to people, and He did not tell them by what name they should address Him if they required assistance in distinguishing between two animals or two plants. Because of this, many troubles arose. There was no one who was capable of resolving the disputes: the questions and the answers never found each other, the air became filled with sentences and nobody knew to whom they belonged, where they came from, or what they wanted. Thus everyone had to furnish his own self with a multiplicity of distinguishing signs."

By the time Lipót Braun had gotten this far in his address, slowly rocking his body back and forth, just as we are doing now, the people sitting in the first rows of the synagogue were whispering vehemently among themselves. What was this all about, that God never said His own name? What kind of beginning was this? God's name was inscribed in the heavens, the names of people were inscribed on the earth. For everything that was in the heavens was set apart, and everything that was on earth was set apart. This Lipót would do better not to overthink everything so much. He'd put his head together with that Salamon again, and now everything was all mixed up. And what were they supposed to make of the reprimand reverberating from the rabbi's words? They hadn't lost the holy words: what before had been on their lips had now migrated into their hearts. And furthermore: Who even knew if Abraham, or Moses, or even David had ever been anything other than a beautiful fabrication, beloved by the ancients? The sons of the ancestors had begun to fear their forefathers, in whom there was still enough strength to replenish all heaven and earth with their wretched hopes, to fill them with their insane devotion; for the ancestors' fear was the same as their love. But no one in the congregation was unruly yet; they were curious to see what would come of this muddle.

If we didn't have to keep our eyes closed, we might discover—inasmuch as would be possible—what happened in the Putnok synagogue on September 12, 1872; and perhaps even now we would see before us the potbelly of Lipót Braun pressing once again against the wooden balustrade of the lectern, looking, for the last time in his life, at the congregation gathered for the High Holy Days, and as he discovers the sympathetic gaze of Salamon Widder, the right corner of his mouth quivers in a bitter smile tending to scorn. But what can we do, my dear friend? We don't see anything, we only hear his voice, sounding out with an ever more crackling sound, as if emerging from the spinning of an old phonograph record: "At that time there lived in the city of Babel a boy and a girl. They were completely alike, and in their childhood nobody could tell them apart. They grew up together, they loved each other, but they were afraid. Yet they were not afraid of the same things as the others. The others were afraid that one day they would wake up not in the same place where they had lain down but in a completely unknown corner of the city, a place they had never been before and the horror of which they had never imagined existing. For here were narrow, dark streets stinking of excrement, people with malicious faces. No one would protect them; their distinguishing marks—a triangle painted on their foreheads, the dots and waves tattooed on their lower arms— would immediately betray that they came from a different, inimical part of the city. The boy and the girl, however, trembled because others in the city wore the same marks as they, and thus one of them could be exchanged with another at any time in such a way that neither of them would ever know. They went therefore one day to the king of Babel and asked him to build a high tower to God; within this tower would be space for every resident of the city, and they would give to God the name of Tower, and there together they would ask Him, in recompense, to name young and old alike, each by a different name, so that everyone would have a name by which they could be addressed. The king was pleased with this idea, and so he had the tower built. When the tower was ready, everyone, with the exception of one old man, came to see it, and they gave God the name of Tower. Then God arose to see what was happening down below because He had never been addressed by any kind of name. He saw the tower, and He burst out laughing, for one entire week He just laughed, because the tower was so tall and the people within were no bigger than ants. And it could be seen that they were really afraid. Then, a week later, when He had grown tired of laughing, He heard the words of the people, and He said, Let it be as you wish. Everyone shall be granted a name, yet they shall not be able to understand each other, because everyone will speak in a different language. And on that day the boy and the girl who had gone to the king lost each other, and the old man who had not gone into the tower died a dreadful death. He was the father of the loving pair."

The Jews of Putnok had had enough. What kind of story was this about Babel? Everyone knew the confusion of languages didn't happen like that. What was this crazy Lipót trying to say? He was ruining the High Holy Days. How could anyone name God "Tower"? What city was he talking about anyway? What was all this supposed to be about—that the people were no bigger than ants, they had no names, and they wrote signs on their forearms? This Lipót had everything all mixed up. Certainly that Salamon had given him something, he had herbs that could make you mad. Lipót Braun should come down from the lectern. My God, what shame! The rabbi of Putnok is crazy. "Lipót, come down!" Salamon Widder whispered this to him from below. "Don't say anything more to them!" But now not only the eyes of Lipót Braun were closed, his ears were closed as well. His body rocked back and forth:

"Ever since then, my dear brothers and sisters, if we pronounce the name of God, we are something like the most wretched of sons who murders his own father and then laments him. But did not everything begin with murder? For Eve gave the name of an unknown father to Abel, saying, 'I have received a son from the Lord,' and as the other aspect of love is dread, without realizing it she had attached a seal to the forehead of her second son, whose name thus became He Who Shall Plunder the Lord. Therefore when Cain said that he did not know where his brother was, he was answering correctly. For one side cannot know about the other. Meaning, however, is never one. That is why God gave Eve two sons at one time, one more than He should have. And these two sons looked at each other like the two halves of a walnut. They were completely the same, and yet they were not the same at all. That is the beginning. That is why King Solomon says, 'I went down to the grove of walnut trees to see the fruits of the valley, and to see whether the vine flourished, and the pomegranates budded.' And the shell of the walnut was immediately broken. The knife was hidden below Cain's mantle; he stabbed Abel, and Abel's blood flowed. And yet what had been two did not become one even after that. Because instead of Abel, another son was born, Seth, whose name means 'substitute.' The two of them remained, but these two resembled each other even less now, because Seth was not in the likeness of God but in the likeness of Adam, and Adam said to Seth: 'God hath granted to me another descendent.' Another—that is to say, not the same. Because nothing can ever be substituted. What is lost is lost for eternity. God did not know this."

With these words, chaos finally broke out. The rabbi was slandering God. From the sound of chairs knocking together we can deduce that at the mention of the name of Cain many in the congregation jumped up, a confused yelling commenced, threats were heard, and by the time Lipót Braun got to the point of saying that God had been mistaken when Seth was born, more than a few congregants were certainly thronging toward the Torah ark, trying to drag Lipót Braun down from there. Then there rang out the cry which made the synagogue of Putnok renowned for decades to come: "We are a dead branch, and the storm which shall smite us down has already awakened!"

That evening Salamon Widder judged it wiser to try to help his friend in his own house. With my great-grandmother's help, they laid him down in the library, and after giving him something which alleviated, to a certain extent, Lipót Braun's labored breathing caused by his angina, he placed an ice-cold compress on his chest, and with my great-grandmother kept watch over him the entire night. At dawn, Lipót Braun awoke feeling as if his bladder were about to burst. My great-grandmother immediately placed the bed-pan, which she had made ready, underneath him, but rather clumsily, it appears, or rather the rabbi was no longer able to direct the liquid pouring out of him, because the bed linens were soaked through; they had to be changed immediately. For this Lipót Braun had to be helped up, and he stood there, so helpless and decrepit in his nightshirt that my great-grandmother, who for her entire life had been a strong healthy woman, displaying no kind of understanding for the weakness of men, felt a wave of anger, also because of the rabbi's clumsiness in soaking the sheets; despite everything, she felt, Mr. Braun shouldn't have let himself go so much. Then the second attack of angina began, clearly much stronger than the first. As there was no physician in Putnok at that time, Salamon Widder tried by his own means to alleviate the rabbi's shortness of breath: he rubbed his chest with ammonium chloride and tried to enlarge the arteries of the heart through massage while my great-grandmother soaked up the cold sweat from the rabbi's brow and the back of his neck with a dry kerchief. It could be seen that they worked excellently together. The pharmacist was reassured by my great-grandmother's fearless, natural strength, to which not only sentimentality but even any understanding of the more refined events of the life of the soul were utterly alien, so much so that he had suspected that behind this mask of willingness to serve lay a profound emotional paralysis and in-sensitivity, which now, however, in the presence of death, requiring only the labor of hands, gave him strength; oth-erwise he would have been prone to despair over the body of his good friend; and yet at the same time he realized that what he had believed to be apathy was in reality something completely different; it was, instead, a kind of trust placed in life—there was no other way to put it—a trust placed in its unknown reserves; and now, as he gazed with gratitude upon this nineteen-year-old peasant girl, in her eternal smell of perspiration, he sensed, for the first time, the fra-grance of a mature woman.

But their exertions could not attain their goal. The rabbi's heart held out against the angina attack not even for an hour. After he had suffered his last, the pharmacist was overcome by fatigue. My great-grandmother remained to help dress the corpse and adjust the clean bed linens around him. At noon they came for him, and two days later the burial was held. As to what happened after this in the pharmacist's house, that I do not know. My great-grandmother remained with him for another two or three months, then she went back to her own village, where she married my great-grandfather. And her stomach immediately began to become round. Seven months after the wedding, my grandfather was born, the father of my father, whom everyone in the village assumed was the son of the pharmacist of Putnok. My great-grandmother became the village healer. The people of the village went to her if they had chest pains, if their spleen ached, if their innards were spasming, and she was called to the women in labor as well: they feared her, because with her resided birth, and with her resided death as well.

3
Things Near and Far Away

Of course, Lipót Braun was right when he said that what is lost is lost forever. But what does it mean to lose something? Does it mean that it has disappeared and is no more, swallowed by the earth, or does it mean only that we don't see it any longer? And if we don't see it, do we even miss it? On the day that Lipót Braun and Salamon Widder were chatting over walnut pastry in the apothecary's house, the pharmacist had the audacity, for the very first time, to intervene in the praxis of his friend. To be precise, when the rabbi reached for the pastry, and could already taste the sweetness of the walnuts in his mouth, Salamon Widder pulled a single tassel from the edge of the carpet, placed it in his pocket, and then asked the rabbi if he thought anything was missing from the carpet. The rabbi examined the carpet, counting the patterns, inspecting each one separately: the stags as they prepared to leap, a leap that is never completed; the doves that seemed to be bending their heads toward the seeds but never reaching them, remaining forever hungry; he inspected the octagonal weaving around these scenes as well, every second pattern enclosing a stag or a dove, the others remaining empty. "No," said the rabbi, "nothing is missing"—for it never once occurred to him to count the tassels.

At that point, Salamon Widder took out the tassel and showed it to Lipót Braun. "This was also in the carpet," he said, "but you didn't notice that it was missing. If you don't know what is missing, you cannot know what is here—or what might turn up from what you thought was lost." And so the rabbi wouldn't forget, Salamon Widder gave him the tassel, tying a knot in it. It seems, though, that the tassel was not intended to remind the rabbi of anything, for what could there have been for him to be reminded of? Wasn't what the four tassels reminded him of, the tassels he wore beneath his waistcoat, enough? Did he need a fifth one as well? Was there so much misfortune in the world that those four tassels couldn't manage it? Lipót Braun shook with laughter at the thought of such impertinence, and as he laughed he rocked back and forth just as when he delivered his homilies from the *bimah*. It should therefore come as no surprise that when he wanted to put the tassel in his pocket—because who knows, maybe this Salamon was right after all, maybe those four tassels were too few, those four that had been sufficient ever since the time of Moses—the tassel dropped to the floor, because what's true is true: the rabbi was very fat and could hardly fit into his trousers, and thus it was very difficult for him to slip such a tiny object as a carpet tassel into his pocket, particularly while laughing. The tassel dropped to the ground, and after the visit my great-grandmother removed it.

And from the house of Salamon Widder nothing else remained, only this memento tassel. And so if we raise it to our ear we can hear what the pharmacist said about the story of Cain. His thoughts about the murderous brother were quite different from the rabbi's. Because it was true that when Cain murdered Abel and stood above his deed, the Lord said to Cain, "Where is your brother Abel?" and Cain answered, "My Lord, I know not." This, in fact, was true. But these were not the words of a murderer: Cain had not yet become one because he still did not know what he had done. How could he have known? For this was the first death in the history of the world. There stood Cain, and there beside him stood the Lord, and neither of them knew what had happened. And the Lord certainly knew even less than Cain, who precisely at that moment sensed something from a great distance: perhaps that death, impossible just a short moment ago—death which meant that either he or his brother, from one moment to the next, could cease to be—was now a possibility.

And as they didn't know what death was, how could they have known, between the two of them, whose was the question and whose the answer? Cain could have asked the Lord, "Where is my brother Abel?" To this, the Lord could have only one reply: "I know not." And if we were to examine the knowledge concealed in this question and answer—for in the end there is knowledge in every question—we come to the realization that Abel is no longer here, and he shall never be here again, or at least not as he was. That moment of "I know not" lost its emptiness even more rapidly than it would have taken Cain or the Lord to utter those three words. By the time they were uttered, the air became filled with accusations; everything became unambiguous. Cain said, "Am I my brother's keeper?" This, accordingly, was also true. And so the time of life continued to flow, just as it had up till then: it flowed onward, no longer completely unconscious; and in the meantime the time of death also shifted, it flowed upward to that place of whose existence we earlier had not the least suspicion.

This is what Salamon Widder said to Lipót Braun on the night they sat together for the last time in the pharmacist's house—or at least that's what one could hear, pressing the tassel up to one's ear—and there was something else as well, but uttered so faintly that I myself don't even know if this is what was said, or if I have only imagined that voice smothered into incoherence by the murmurings of the years. In any event, Salamon Widder most likely did say something about how it was a great thing—even a source of inexhaustible hope—that the first murder occurred between two brothers. Because it is only between siblings that the roles and the questions can be exchanged. When Cain said that he didn't know where Abel was, the Lord Himself didn't even know—and we ourselves don't even know—but then suddenly he came upon the answer, as he had to, and because he came upon it, he was compelled to remain silent before the Lord, and no one saw where Abel was, because he was already inside Cain.

With this beautiful, truly hopeful utterance, Salamon Widder withdrew from the world, but not every trace of him disappeared. Because there are places where memory sees far. The village to which my great-grandmother moved was encircled by the Bükk Mountains. An overgrown path led from the ridge of the mountain to its peak, from which you could see all the way to Putnok. You could see the house of the Jewish apothecary, and Rabbi Lipót Braun as well, his body swaying back and forth as he gave his homily about Babel; you could see the golden-brown mounds of the walnut pastry, sprinkled with powdered sugar; and you could see that my grandfather really was the son of the Jewish apothecary of Putnok.

But since to look across to Putnok is different from looking at the mossy, blackened thatched roof directly opposite, the house pulling it down over its eyes like the old women pulling down their kerchiefs, and since the fog and humid darkness often settle upon the Bükk Mountains all the way up to the ridge, the one who remembers can easily become lost in the darkness of days, especially if his eyes are straining to see. At such times, the village closes in on itself, its trees invaded by crows: their echoing caws fill the widening silence, and whatever is far sinks into oblivion like a piece of wood saturated with water; what is near slips into the place of the faraway; what happened yesterday seems to have occurred years ago. As far as the villagers were concerned, if at one time my grandfather had been the son of the Jewish apothecary, then my father was also Jewish—and onto that, as with everything else, a thick layer of white snow settled in the course of the years.

Because what does it mean to be Jewish in a village where no one has ever seen a Jew? Above all, what does it mean if the Jew isn't even a Jew, but just as stout and real as we ourselves—here he is, taking huge bites out of his bread with bacon boiled with garlic, which he holds with a tiny piece of bread crust so he can tear off thin slices. He takes the pretty, rose-pink fat from the knife blade into his mouth, his mustache leaps up and down as he eats, his fingers are shiny from grease and paprika; he is not at all like those veil-sheathed, faraway things—so easy to forget, and, as you can see, already they have been swallowed up by the fog.

There lived once in Prague a rabbi who declared that as the Jews wander in the fog of the millennia it remains undecided if they will perish in the dark mists or reach the Jaffa gates in Jerusalem, where, beneath an arcade, a wretched beggar sits on a small footstool. His body sways back and forth, a dark upwelling of laughter keeps bursting out of him. What is the beggar laughing at? Speak to him, ask him! He will say that he is laughing at you, for he is the Angel of the Last Day. Don't believe him, though! If you feel no darkness could be thicker, do not be afraid; know that this darkness has absorbed into itself the most radiant light. Then your heart will be filled with mercy for the beggar, and he will cease his rocking and laughing. And now ask him, upon his soul, what he is waiting for. He will say he has been waiting for you, and only for you is he waiting. And now you should believe him! Believe him, because this means everyone will become their mistakes—and the biggest mistake of the Jew is that he doesn't know how to tarry like a beggar next to the Angel of the Last Day but must go on wandering and getting lost. He must lose the name of God within his own self.

Yet it was not possible to see all the way to Prague, where the rabbi gave his homily, from the peak of the Bükk Mountains, however high they were. Might it then be possible to see that far from the concrete top of the covered well in my grandmother's courtyard, where I often clambered up? I sat upon the well's warm concrete roof, while below me the geese pecked away at the mulberry tree's sweet black fruit; they couldn't get enough of it, just as I couldn't get enough of the view, not only of things close by, the things all around myself—inasmuch as the colossal mulberry tree next to the first house afforded me a good view of the village—but also of the faraway things that appeared behind my closed eyelids as I sat perched on the well's roof. Of course I shouldn't have been climbing up there; it would have been so easy to slip, and the well was deep; it always took so long to let the bucket down. But I didn't worry about that, just as the inhabitants of the village didn't worry about how far away Jerusalem was or whether a beggar sat on his footstool next to the Jaffa Gate, laughing as he rocked back and forth.

The Jew is a mistake. The Jew is the one you don't give your daughter to. And yet my father was able to get the woman he loved. But how he did this I will reveal only after I've told you what I saw from the burning concrete roof of the well.

I saw what was near, and I saw the borders of faraway things. I saw the half-circle of the Bükk Mountains with their tall oaks, which were close but still not close enough for the people to run into the forest when the Tatars, with their shrieking yelps, attacked the village from the south. And who were these people fleeing into the forest? They were Czechs and Germans. Their memory is preserved in the names: the Pohorka meadow, the Nemecke valley, the Dobra oak forest. This is where they herded their pigs to feed upon acorns. And if one of them had survived the Tatar rampage, once he dared to venture out of the forest, he wouldn't have glanced back even once at the smoldering cinders of the beams. The village lay in ruins. But it did not remain unpopulated for long. Slovaks came to take the place of the Czechs and the Germans, and they married Hungarian brides, quickly becoming Magyarized themselves. They had to render military service to the cathedral chapter in

Eger; the men were present during the siege of Eger in 1552. One of them, Ádám Fürjes, was commemorated in Géza Gárdonyi's novel *Eclipse of the Crescent Moon*. Yet when the dust swirled up from the road in the wake of the marauders of the Beg of Fülek, no one was insane enough to take a stand and fight them. They ran into the forest, but once again the forest was too far away. Everyone beyond the shallows was slaughtered; their bodies lay pell-mell in the tall grass. The sun scorched, the horseflies dug their crooked legs into the skin of the dead, and by evening, when the air had cooled somewhat, the meadow was driven mad by the chirruping of crickets. For beyond the shallows lay the hayfields—the crickets' land.

And I saw the roads that lead from everywhere into the village, from Sáta, Csernely, Várkony, Somsály, Gárdony, Lénárddaróc—all like veins into the middle of an opened palm. The center of the palm was the square in front of the church, bordered on the opposite side by the inn and the bull stables. I saw the men as they set off, armed with their scythes so the residents of Várkony in the Corpus Christi procession crossing the fields would know for whom the Szurdo vineyards bore their fruit. I didn't see the Szurdo vineyards, though, because the Várkony land, after the death of the last of the Bárius family, ended up in the possession of the noble Vays, whose property was confiscated by the Habsburg Imperial Chamber for their part in Rákóczi's uprising; the proud Vays not only bought their property back at a high price but acquired the Szurdo vineyards from the Eger cathedral chapter as well. Instead of the vineyards, though, I saw the old church, consecrated in the name of Our Lady in the year when the French and the Austrians, battling each other in the Rhineland, finally sat down to talks in Vienna, and divided up Italy between Sicily and Sardinia as well as deciding on the fate of Lothringia, and in doing so, it appeared, removed all obstacles in the way of Maria Theresa's coronation. Yet this peace was short-lived; for it took no longer than five years for all of Europe's armies to reassemble, so the old church consecrated to Our Lady did not remain standing for long: it was destroyed by fire. I don't know what made that church burst into flames. But to seek the cause of fire is not necessary. For what is time itself but fire, reducing everything to ashes, so that it may cede its place to something else. Thus the new church was built on the site of the old, its tower now thicker, stouter. And I saw other men, no longer with scythes in their hands but carbide lamps, as they set off at the break of dawn across the Bükk Mountains to Pereces and Bánfalva, then to Farkaslyuk, to the mineshafts. The carbide was jolted around in the lamp's lower chamber; water sloshed in the upper one. When the valve was opened, water dripped into the carbide chamber, forming gas released through a tube to the burner. The carbide lamps burned with a beautiful white light.

And I saw the crosses alongside the road. A thin strip of tinplate arched above them to protect them from the rain, they were surrounded by a low fence, and the body of Jesus, cut from tinplate as well, was nailed to the wood. Drawn and painted Jesuses, faceless because the faces and the eyes had been eaten away by rust. The bells toll into paradise, all the angels round the cross, till the midnight hour comes, after midnight for all time, till the break of dawn. Rusty, rain-streaked Jesus bodies with no face. Only the loincloth remained white and the halo yellow. I walk out before my own gate, gaze upward into the heights of heaven, and there I see a golden chapel, therein lies a golden throne. The crosses were erected by well-to-do families out of gratitude because their sons had come home from the front, or in mournful remembrance because they had perished there. There stood the Szalmás cross, the Fónagy cross, the Vargás cross, the Kaló cross, and the Susó cross. Fortune and misfortune, miraculous healings and sudden deaths: all left a uniform sign. And beneath the crosses, as in the cemeteries, were gathered torn bits of ribbon, dried flowers. No one ever removed them. Arise, Peter, to the black earth, proclaim this small prayer! The crosses stood there, and that was enough. When villagers departed upon a long journey, no one bid them farewell, when they returned no one greeted them. But if a storm might cause one of the crosses to break, if a bolting horse might pull its cart over one of them, or if one evening the crosses might simply disappear, then a new and unknown fear would creep into the villagers' hearts. The villagers might have gone farther along those roads: they would have gone up to Sáta, to Csernely, to Várkony, Somsály, Gárdony, Lénárddaróc, and even farther than that, all the way up to Ózd, but they couldn't trust the road anymore, because who can trust a road where a cross has fallen down? They would no longer have any trust in the world—or themselves. They would have become like the Jews. Knowing that the roads lead nowhere. They go on, they go on, but they don't lead anywhere—which is to say they lead precisely nowhere.

And yet nowhere is not the place of annihilation. If someone goes to nowhere, then there is already nothing more to cremate, nothing more to break apart in him, nothing more to be taken away. Because in the final analysis, the only thing that can be taken away from a person is his face. Nowhere is the land of desolation we wander across. There everything is born and dies in the same way, flourishes and wilts—in a word, everything lives there in the same way, but more vividly, than in somewhere; everything has a body, a smell, a closeness and a distance, only time does not pass, and as for things happening, nothing ever happens; eyes do not see and ears do not hear. Everything stands there in the same place, the most insensate grasshopper, even the last blade of grass: all stand at the gates of an imaginary, wished-for land; they have already renounced the possibility of ever gaining entry. But even so they cannot move, and in that nowhere they disappear without ever having known the tranquillity of death. They float upward like smoke, like the mists of dawn. Here in this place is where the Jews live. And it was from this place that my father escaped when Judge Susó prepared his identity papers: where the grandfather's name was supposed to be recorded, the name of Salamon Widder, the Jewish apothecary, was not written down—that would have pushed my father one step farther into that nowhere—instead, the word *unknown* was written. And that also was true because no one knew who Salamon Widder was anymore, no one remembered him, as in actuality, there wasn't really anything to remember. His ominous beginnings were attributed, but perhaps only by the wagging tongues of the village, to the fact, stirring the imagination but all the more disturbing for that, that my great-grandmother, who had a mysterious knowledge of herbs and illnesses, and who arrived in the village husbandless but with a boy child in her belly, was received warmly by the village's Jewish families; her son—my grandfather—spent as much time at the houses of the butcher and the grocer as if he'd been born there. He knew without explanation what to do when the Sabbath came, for without him the lights of the Holy Day would have remained an unhappy glimmer; his task for the two Jewish families was to warm up the *cholent,* cooked on Friday mornings, in the oven, to take logs from the woodpile and place them on the fire. And even if Salamon Widder had existed, if these ill-omened origins had not arisen from the imaginings of a village in search of secrets, the apothecary still would have long ago belonged among those who vanish into nowhere without a trace; even his name would drift upward like the wreathing vapor of cholent made with plenty of eggs and thickened with barley. If I myself do not take hold of that vapor on which the name of my grandfather is written, if I do not hold a sheet of paper above the aromatic cholent in the ceramic dish, made from a recipe handed down, as Heinrich Heine believed, to Moses from God, then I shall not be able to tell the story carried by that life for the last time, and—as I recollect it now—perhaps borne yet even today.

Salamon Widder's name alone would not, of course, have been enough to propel my father, Nándor Józsa, into nowhere. The Third Anti-Jewish Law of August 1941—if not exactly dispelling all doubts and, with its many exceptions, lagging behind German practice for a time—finally and precisely mandated who should be regarded as a Jew, just as precisely as such a delicate matter could be mandated. Not lacking in this definition was a permissive, nearly culpable, even magnanimous tolerance. Anyone with two grandparents born into the Israelite denomination must be considered Jewish. Two grandparents. One half of the ancestors.

There are cases, however, and there are times in which one is not any less than two. And this is precisely the case of the Jews, and it is precisely our time that necessitates the realization of a new concept in view of obsolete laws insufficiently serving the national interest. Because what does the Jew do? He betrays you. It's enough for you to close your eyes for a second; the Jew has already wrangled everything for his own family, his own business—your past and your future belong to him; when he grabs the corner of something he never lets it go. Like the eagle, he devours your seed corn. And so the question regarding the Jew is not whether there is one or two of them, but whether there is any Jew at all. The law has not been enacted for you to consider the exceptions but for you to enforce it even where patience has made room for its own errors.

The memory of Salamon Widder, though, was expunged without a trace before the eyes of strangers by that wondrous word *unknown*. My father didn't have to bother with the Jewish fears that nailed them down to history. "As for man, his days are as grass: as a flower of the field, so he flourisheth. For the wind passeth over it, and it is gone; and the place thereof shall know it no more." The villagers also sang the lines of the Psalms, but for them the words meant something different. They were not filled with dread because the world always belonged to others, and always would. They made no distinction among the old things: for them everything happened yesterday. The Tatars arrived yesterday, Balázs Ományi fell at Mohács yesterday, the Turks from Fülek overran the village yesterday, the hajduks, foot soldiers of Rákóczi, also passed through here yesterday; it was yesterday when new languages were heard in the depopulated village: a question asked in Czech was answered in German, a courtship in Slovak was rebuffed in Hungarian. And it was yesterday too that a dead man came back from the war. They did not need these fears to know that the short life of one individual can be expunged from eternity without a single trace—to know whether a person may for a short while receive something that does not pass away, for it is written, "One generation passeth away, and another cometh, but the earth abideth for ever." Here fear dictated where the borders of the village were drawn. Those of the men were far away, by the entrance to the mines; those of the women closer, where the crosses stood; and the children's even closer still, along the fence.

And strange, chilling things happened at these borders. I knew the closest ones, the children's fears, the best. I saw from the roof of the well as Ilonka Bóna came home from the vineyards. She was a handsome young woman, with strong legs and a strong chest. As it was a hot summer day, Ilonka stopped beside a path and pulled her skirt up to her thighs to fan herself a little. The rainwater running down from the mountain washed the lanes, their deep paths impassable and overgrown with shrubbery, into the loamy earth. And so it was, but then out from the shrubbery, as if waiting just for this moment, a wild boar came bursting forth. The hem of the skirt fell, and Ilonka in her terror scarcely dared move. The boar was between her legs. What should she do now? If she moved, the boar would bite her loin. "Go back into the thickets," she whispered to him. But the boar had no intention of going anywhere. Instead, he began to caress Ilonka's shin with his body, so pleasurably that her skin rose in goosebumps. Now Ilonka stamped her foot on the ground and ordered the boar to go back into the shrubbery and never come out again. The boar, however, as if understanding the meaning of her words, began to nudge in between Ilonka's legs, but with such a delicacy as not even a young countess could dream of. Ilonka then started off with the boar under her skirt. When she reached home, she put the boar in the pigsty. Her husband was glad; he didn't even ask where it had come from. Later, when Ilonka gave birth to a boy, its entire body was covered in wild bristles. Ghastly, horrifying. Ilonka wrapped her son, the little crying piglet, in swaddling clothes, and threw him into the thicket, in exactly the same place where the boar had run out. It was evening, so no one saw anything. But whoever has an ear can discern, even today, the piglet-weeping of Ilonka Bóna's infant son coming from the overgrown paths.

And what else does that person hear? What stories? For stories, in the final analysis, are not for eyes. On the contrary. Anyone who steps into the world begs for stories and would gladly sit upon every stone where a story is being told, would take a seat in every tavern, wander around the marketplace, not to be given food and drink but to gather up time. For the longest-lived person is the one who has heard the most stories. And whoever lives for a long time realizes in due course that it is better to lose one's sight. The world of yesterday will become desolate and uninhabited as the calendar marks another day. Even the eye can see only what is there, and what is there never exists longer than a single moment. Impoverished memory tries in vain to make this moment longer. How many have danced in attendance upon matters of memory, and all so futile! The stones are smashed apart, the canvases grow battered, paper burns.

But just stand somewhere on a street corner and listen with ears open to the people who always, even today, incessantly tell stories; they relate their own tales and within them is everything. Or if no one is nearby, if you have awakened in a godforsaken place, it is enough to sit up on the roof of the well, to climb a tree, or simply to open your window so that with eyes closed you can listen into the distance. Stories will float toward you from every direction.

I too sat like that on the roof of the well, I closed my eyes: the mountain ridge, the dark roofs, the fences all disappeared, and above my head the air became filled with the din of birds. Below, from the swampy meadow where blue will-o'-the-wisps fluttered came the shrieking of the sandpipers and the voices of the reed buntings. Where the road forks in two, the frog settlement tittered and chattered the entire day. To slip into one of the deep retting pools was a more terrifying death than any child could have ever imagined, and yet the children happily played there, jumping from the shore onto the hemp rafts weighted down by stones and attached to stakes battered into the bottom of the lake. Perhaps they were brave because there were so many other ways for them to die. High fevers, night demons, poisonous mushrooms, the adder's vicious bites, the enticements of the Gypsies. The birds from below, the sandpipers, the green plovers, the black-chested reed buntings knew their names, they knew who had died, they knew when and how. The swampy meadow swallowed up their small bodies and often only gave them back weeks later, swollen with gases and putrid. At such times, the Gypsies were asked to pull out the unfortunate children's bodies with sticks and leave them on the edge of the meadow where the putrid vapors could be released, their gases escaping.

The birds above, the swallows alighting on the mulberry tree, knew of other deaths. Of long, tedious illnesses and endless complaints. They settled only in courtyards where instead of seeing into the darkened rooms they peered deep into the hearts of young people, and although I doubt they understood too much of these hearts' hope-filled accounts, they still debated potential matches all day long, and since the bride or groom was almost never the one of their choosing, there was, subsequently, much to discuss: who had ruined their own lives and been wed when they should have run far away. Every time I climbed up to the well roof, an entire flock of sparrows flew up from the valley, covering the mulberry tree, and it hummed as they chirped out the stories, continually interrupting the other's words.

"Your mother was a pretty girl, didn't you know that?"

"They raised her like a little lady from the town."

"She went to school in shoes."

"And later on, she even got a sewing machine."

"The girls came to her to have their dresses sewn."

"So she would trim their trousseaus."

"And she did Richelieu embroidery for them too."

"They didn't love each other at all."

"Because they never sat outside on the little bench chatting."

"Of course they did. She was just different from the rest of them."

"That's why she had suitors, and not just one."

"Rich peasant boys."

"If you own at least ten *holds* of land, I'll take you; that's what she always said."

"She wouldn't have taken anyone because she was ill."

"Every true story begins with an illness."

"With an illness or a crime."

"Your mother's illness began like this: she had no bowel movements."

"Not even for a week, she simply didn't need it."

"She ate plum preserves, though. Spooned them into her mouth from the pot."

"But her intestines didn't even churn."

"She knew she'd be in terrible pain again."

"That her intestines would bleed."

"It's a miracle she didn't get blood poisoning."

"She withdrew and purged herself with chamomile and potassium permanganate."

"She said she'd never have a husband."

"Then your father came along."

"He was very good looking. He even performed in the folklore troupe."

"It's just that he was Jewish. Jakub, Jakub."

"Of course he wasn't, even his father wasn't, he was properly baptized."

"That wasn't the problem with him. The problem was he liked to talk, not to work."

"You're spreading that rumor as well?"

"I'm not spreading it. I can keep quiet, but still it was true."

"His older brothers lived a Gypsy life. One of them divorced three times, and in the meantime he traveled all across America. What could your grandmother have liked about that?"

"Then when your father became a soldier, not a hair on his head was harmed in Serbia or the Carpathians, but he nearly perished at the Dnieper."

"Even you felt the grenade shards in his shoulder and back."

"His eyes were operated on. He nearly went blind."

"And your father's older sister, Margit Józsa, went to your great-grandmother's house, saying, Who was going to love her little Nandi now?"

"Your mother said that the one who loved him until now would continue to do so, but just so she wouldn't have to listen to Margit's endless complaining anymore."

"And now at least, both of them were sick."

"And we put them together."

"We fixed them up together."

"We chirped upon the tree."

"And your father, all the same, didn't understand anything, but he said to your mother that he would cure her."

"And from that point on, your mother complained for the next fifty years that she was stuck with a wistful, useless man, but still in her own way she loved him."

"And your father was silent."

"Only once he said something to the effect that even a horse needs to be caressed."

"And Erzsi was immediately cured of her troubles as well."

"As if she'd never even been ill."

"Nothing of the kind! She had to work so hard around the house, and then in the vineyards, she had no time for illness."

And so the sparrows chirped away in the mulberry tree. But sparrows are foolish creatures. They chatter and chatter back and forth, whether they need to or not. Their beaks never stop. The silence of the infinite spaces frightens them. If every other being were to fall mute, they would always be the ones to start up, filling all creation from one corner to the next with their voices. In this way they are similar to the angels. And all the while, ever since time began, the angels, heads bent forward and knees drawn up, have been plunging down below, carrying unharmed within themselves the sense that they and only they are at home in time, as they fill it with talk of wars, marriages, enticements, and deceptions. Yet a human being—whether it is good for him or not—listens to the murmurings of the angels and slowly, like children who remain attached to the images of waking life, falls asleep.

4

A Present for Father Dolphus

There were Christians in Denkendorf, where Master Fröschlin was my kindhearted and patient teacher; although these Christians were in no way as peaceful as in other locales. Of course, this was not surprising in a city whose temperament had been so recently agitated by strife, although outwardly everything appeared to show the greatest picture of calm—one heard only infrequently of violent trespass and murder taking place, and as a rule the perpetrators' identities were quickly revealed. Such apparent calm, however, could not deceive me. I immediately sensed the weight of fear in the air; fear has the weight of a thick, ominous cloud heralding an imminent storm, even though the wind has not arisen, even though the sequence of misfortunes has yet to begin.

It was a long time, however, before I suspected that the house of Master Fröschlin had anything to do with this fear. It is true that few cared for him in the city; he did not have any friends to speak of, and behind the market square, where the cobblers' street begins, one of his "well-wishers," someone whom he had previously insulted, would incite the street urchins, always game for anything, against him. These street brats would surround him and, babbling, hollering, and guffawing, pelt him with wild chestnuts and horse manure, while he, with his short legs, stumbled and tripped trying to avoid the painful and stinking projectiles. Master Fröschlin did not seem to take such matters too seriously, however: "Pay no mind," he would mutter to himself, "they need some kind of amusement"—and I myself explained such events along the same reasoning, as surely things are easy for physicians nowhere. For as in any small city, there was in Denkendorf an innumerable horde of charlatans—root-gathering women, blacksmiths, Sunday market criers, hunters—all recommending their own healing ointments and other wares to the public, with even the magistrate, Mr. Gabe, passing himself off as a learned doctor; people who were in some kind of trouble not only trusted the cures of these common thieves more than any physician's implements, they even trusted a crazy shepherd's cures more—although for these latter, every illness had but one cure: to fleece the patient as much as possible.

In addition, Master Fröschlin, with his appearance, rather deserved to be shunned. He was an ugly man, truly ugly, as if nature, that most talented of caricaturists, were practicing its skills on him; for as nature is attracted, in a divine manner, to the frailty of the weak, it also, by way of recompense, abundantly gifted the ugly Master Fröschlin with a good and even temperament. Thus, when, with his undulating gait, which was all his short legs permitted him, he appeared at the market, entering the square from the cobblers' street to select some cheese or vegetables (as he never entrusted this to Mistress Agnete), he could be sure that no matter what he might choose the market purveyors would, owing to their imperceptible sleight of hand, give him the rottenest head of lettuce and the driest hunk of cheese; but at this he just laughed. His ugliness gave him leave to please only himself and not the common folk in any way, and he never permitted his mood to be ruined. That a more concealed bitterness had settled in the depths of his soul, as at the bottom of a good casket of wine, was betrayed precisely by this good humor, which often manifested itself in a kind of boorish, albeit unconscious and unintentional, sarcasm, even when inadvisable. At the market, for example, I myself one day heard him, as he addressed an honorable lady who, as was commonly known, was hoping for a child from the midwife's tablets (and not from her impotent husband), asking her why she did not speak instead to the first young lad she might see, as he could certainly supply a prescription for her trouble, and indeed the healing might bring her some pleasure; afterward there would be plenty of time to send for the old witch.

In short, Master Fröschlin laughed at the residents of Denkendorf; as long as he could do so, he had the strength to deal with them. Secretly though, he still hoped for their acceptance, because otherwise why would he have immediately gone running over to the house of the Reverend Martin Dolphus, prior of the monastery, as soon as it came to his knowledge that that honorable gentleman was suffering from a powerful ailment of the stomach and abdomen, which was otherwise not too peculiar, as his housekeeper cooked for him well and abundantly? Master Fröschlin made me swear on my soul that I would make haste in delivering a small bottle to the prior in which there was an infusion of bloodwort, well known for its beneficial effects on the stomach. And I did take the infusion over to him, although I did not hurry; instead, I took a detour toward the bakery, where I often stopped in, and not only because of the fine plum pastries. Not too long after, a letter arrived stating that Father Dolphus was very grateful for the remedy, and that he would be more than happy to receive Master Fröschlin as a guest.

My master did not delay. He conveyed his reply immediately, not forgetting to include a gift. He sent me with a larger bottle of the same infusion, in case there might be need of it, and he sent a rare cross as well. He knew that the prior had a beautiful collection of all manner of valuable objects, and he hoped that with such a rare piece as this he might come closer to his heart. He did not suspect that the opposite would happen: that instead, he was hastening his own ruination.

The house of the prior was on the monastery grounds. Two tall oak trees stood before it; the loud clack of the ram-headed knocker on the gate announced one's presence. The prior opened the door to my knocking himself and bade me enter in an amiable manner; after I gave him the letter with the present, he remarked that he was just about to dine; insofar as I was here already he would be very glad not to have to take his meal alone. He put down the gift without unwrapping or looking at it, then, with the gesture of a teacher toward a favored pupil, clasped my shoulder and accompanied me to table. As we took our places, the cook placed a platter of well-roasted leg of veal on a bed of pickled porcini mushrooms before us; the prior first cut me a thick slice of veal, then an even thicker slice for himself, pouring out two glasses of fine wine as well, and he commenced his meal with an ostentatious devotion which I had never observed in him as he busied himself around the altar table of the death and resurrection of Christ Our Lord. I myself followed his example, and I must confess that never had I eaten as well in my life as I did at the house of Father Dolphus. It seemed that whoever said that if Christ was the Redeemer of souls, he was certainly not the redeemer of stomachs, was correct; and so his suffering meant nothing.

When the prior had abated the first hunger of his irredeemable stomach, he began to tell a story which he had recently read in an extremely wise book—as it was well known that he gladly read such stories, he would now tell it to me, curious to hear my thoughts—let him see if in reality I was as sharp-witted a boy as people said I was. The story went like this:

"Once upon a time there lived a powerful king somewhere in Arabia. From his many wives were born countless sons and daughters, and he loved them all the same, but among his sons, there was one, Abadon, whom he favored more than all the others, and he overlooked his faults. Abadon had a younger sister, the beautiful Danila. The queen, however, was not the mother of Abadon, but the mother of Emunis, who himself had for a long time been in love with Danila, though he did not betray his secret to anyone. So tortured was he by love that he grew thin and pale.

"'What is wrong with Prince Emunis?' a friend of his asked him. 'If you say what oppresses your heart, you will feel relieved, and perhaps I can help you.'

"Emunis told the truth to his friend, who advised him to lie down on his bed as if very ill and allow no one near him except his most faithful servants. Then he should make himself ever more ill and weak, taking neither food nor drink, until the king came to him and asked how he might be healed. And when the king came, he should ask them to send to him the beautiful Danila, for her cooking might taste better to him.

"And so it happened, and when the beautiful Danila came to Emunis and took the food over to the bed of her ailing sibling, Emunis began to implore her, 'Lie down next to me, or I shall die.' Of course, Danila was greatly frightened, and she said, 'Do not wish for such dreadful things.' Emunis, however, would not hear what Danila was saying: he embraced her, but after he was able to carry out his plan, he began to feel loathing for Danila, and he called his servants to chase her away from the house.

"Danila wept bitterly, and she told Abadon what had happened. The king also found out, and his anger was inflamed against Emunis, but the queen pacified him. Within Abadon the desire for revenge burned, and a goodly time later he organized a great hunt to which he also invited his princely siblings. During the dinner, his servants threw themselves upon Emunis and murdered him. The king then cursed Abadon and ordered him never again to cross the threshold of his palace.

"Then Abadon gathered many people around him to incite an uprising against his father, with whom only a few had remained. Thus, a few days later he seized the city and dishonored all the king's concubines. The king, disguised, was able to escape in time, but among his remaining servants, many abandoned him, pelting him with stones and mocking him. Those who had remained with him wished to set off against Abadon immediately, even if it meant being ripped apart by him and his men. The king did not hold them back; he did, however, say, 'As my own son, who hails from my own body, is the one who has committed this deed, all of this has occurred because of my own sin.'

"And although the king's servants were far fewer in number, great confusion and fear arose among the armies of Abadon; Abadon himself fled, but the king's men overtook him and stabbed him.

"And when the king learned of this, in his sadness he wandered away to the desert, never to return. And the people said, 'If only all of us had died, and if only Abadon had remained alive, now surely he would be rejoicing here in his palace.'

"And so life went on in the city, and they never saw the king again."

The prior told the story, and I did not dare answer; what could I have said, if for once, surprising my own self, I felt sympathy for that crazy Emunis who was in love with his own sister, and I also understood why he ended up loathing Danila after he was finally able to embrace her: it was because he could not embrace her for all eternity. Abadon had only been doing what Emunis wanted to do when he murdered him, and the king's servants did what Abadon wanted them to do. "Oh, poor, poor king," I finally said, instead of pronouncing these reflections to the prior, because if I had tested the mettle of my stomach at his table with these chosen delicacies, I was indeed obliged to say something. It appeared that he was satisfied with my answer. He pushed the leg of veal, gleaming with juices on the bed of porcini mushrooms, over toward me, urging me to take another helping, but warned me not to fall victim to the greediness of a hungry person, as the marinated fish with almonds and the cheese soufflé were still waiting their turn in the kitchen. Not only had I never even eaten such foods before; Master Fröschlin too was unacquainted with them, not even by hearsay.

Therefore, a week later, when the two of us went again to the monastery, Master Fröschlin was full of hope, as he was of the opinion that if the prior had served me such a sumptuous dinner, now for the two of us he would certainly conjure up the table of Solomon; and he secretly hoped as well that he might be offered the position of monastery physician which had been vacant for a long time. My poor master, however, was to be disappointed in both his hopes.

This time, the housekeeper of Father Dolphus received us with scanty fare. Before us she placed some half-raw, greasy roast pork in a suspicious-looking yellow sauce, bitter as bile. I merely poked at the meat with the tip of my knife, broke off bits of bread, and drank wine with it; Master Fröschlin, however, honorably set about his meal, although he could not completely suppress his repulsion bordering on nausea, swallowing with difficulty, eyes squinting and lower lips turned down. In contrast, the prior ate with gusto, bathing the thick pink chunks of meat in the ill-smelling, bitter gravy with evident pleasure, like someone who in that moment had no other business anywhere in the world or heaven, and as if by consuming this meal he were doing everything to remedy the ills of the destitute: he wiped the corner of his mouth with satisfaction.

And yet even with this, our epigastric tortures—with which Father Dolphus appeared to be punishing the devil that lived within us, who of course merits every punishment—had not yet come to an end. And Father Dolphus, observing our suffering from beginning to end, leaning back in his armchair after dinner with satisfaction, commanded us to now place our hopes in the pastry, in the fine dough which was now rising, just as the unleavened soul rises from the yeast of mercy. As concerned pastry, however, he continued, in his house there were strict rules. In order to better illuminate this pause—just as we do not read the holy lesson by the mass table—it would be advisable to sanctify that of which the greedy body no longer has need, namely tastes and forms, those things we may imbibe with the pure and slow pleasure of creation, in another location, and in this house there was no more suitable place than the second floor, for just as we lift our hearts, we must also lift our bodies to receive the greatest possible grace on their behalf.

The staircase was steep and made of dark wood. Poor Father Dolphus huffed and puffed so much that he needed to stop for a rest after a few steps. He leaned on the banister with all his weight, the blood rushing to his face.

"What a wise thing," he sighed, "that salvation does not await the body"; and after a short pause, he added, his countenance overcast: "Do you hear me, gentlemen, I speak of the church of God, from which the good soul must, at one point, be forcibly cast out, just as Jesus cast out the demons in the form of pigs from the demon-possessed."

As to his meaning we did not have much time to ponder because upstairs we found ourselves among genuine treasures. There was a carved inlaid wooden sideboard; there were panoramic views of German, Dutch, and French cities showing towers, steeply roofed houses, and market squares. From the shelter given by a corner house on a broad square, itself embraced by pretty houses in a half-arc, a tall, gangly man steps out, wearing black stockings and black trousers; below his shoulder he carries a large wooden box with many compartments. Who is he? Is he a cynical, aged bachelor, thought to be dry and boring by the others? Or on the contrary, is he an adventurous young boy, a baker of French pâtés who has found an abundant living in Germany? Oh, the story had already formed in my head. Four French boys, all of them from Paris: one a language tutor, another a fencing master, the third a dancing master, and the pâté maker already known to us, all set out in their younger years to Berlin, having formed a tightly knit friendship when the diligence brought them together. Fate was kind to them: they were as one soul and one body. With the completion of the day's work, they spent every evening together, and as befits true Frenchmen, their conversation was lively, the meal moderate. With the passage of years, however, the legs of the dancing master became sluggish, the arm of the fencing master lost its vigor in old age, the language tutor was surrounded by rivals boasting of their knowledge of the latest French expressions, and the clever discoveries of the pâté maker were surpassed by newer delicacies. Thus the foursome abandoned their business ventures, and after getting over the sadness of unfortunate times, the dancing and fencing masters paid a visit to their old pupils, now retired officers of high rank, chamberlains, stewards; as they had moved in the highest of circles, they collected all the news of the day so that the conversation should not flag. The language master scoured the shelves of the antiquarian's bookshop searching for French volumes filled with language the Académie would approve of, the pâté maker took care of all the cooking.

There was another picture as well. In it, a man wearing a leather apron was piling sacks from a cart next to a mill on the banks of a river, while a bit farther on a hot-headed woman was lecturing a young girl; farther down, fish were about to be unloaded from a fishing boat. What could the hot-headed woman be saying to that poor girl? As I stared at the picture, I felt she could hardly be teaching her anything other than the art of thrift, as is always the wont of wealthy burghers, soap makers, or the fat and rather homely daughters of indigo dyers. The hand of that woman—along with all the other corresponding parts—had been won by a modest private secretary, and now all she did from morning to night was economize so as to blame that poor private secretary for everything, although he was to blame for nothing.

Father Dolphus informed us of how he had come to acquire every picture, statue, and piece of furniture, and how much he had paid for them. To my great surprise, my master was well versed in these objects, his inquiries no cause for shame. I had no idea where he could have acquired such knowledge of the various kinds of wood, of the nature of these materials, of the work of carpenters and painters, and I perceived immediately that his fears, owing to which I had nearly had to hold him up on the way to the monastery, had completely dissipated and that the prior was also enjoying the discussion.

I had never imagined that the painting of a picture would demand so much expertise, and that so much mystery resided in the different varieties of wood. It was not, however, a picture that elicited the greatest pride from Father Dolphus but rather a book, as he placed it before us. Titled *Augustinus,* it was published by Jacobus Zegers in Leuven in 1640:

on the title page it depicted Saint Augustine, the apostle of mercy, with a burning flame in his left hand and in his right hand a quill and codex; with his foot, he trampled down the head of Pelagius, the cursed heretic who refused to abandon his claim that man is not a corrupted being and divine grace is unneeded to become righteous; therefore the sacrifice of Jesus was in vain. Oh, unhappy man, how could he have scraped together so much blind love and trust toward the world? Had he not seen murder and crime one thousand-fold? And yet what if, despite this, man would be good, and Pelagius—who was later expelled from Jerusalem and died in one of the forgotten corners of the wide East—would be the chief, indeed perhaps the only, saint among all human beings whose feet had ever worn away the soil of this earth?

Pelagius, Pelagius, I murmured his name to myself as the prior led us into the windowless back room. Here only dim light filtered in from the neighboring chamber. In the middle of the table a platter of pastry had already been set out. Father Dolphus bade us sit down in two armchairs; from the wall above a cardinal looked down upon us with eyes that nearly stabbed human flesh; surely this gaze alone was proof that the good Pelagius had been mistaken. As we sat down, the prior immediately served us dessert. On the platter was walnut pastry, but so dry that it set my teeth on edge, and by the time I was able to break off a piece and chew on it, it had practically no taste.

Luckily, my tortures attracted no attention. The conversation between the prior and my surgeon master continued on lighter subjects, and as emerged quickly from their chit-chat, the art of cheerful mockery was hardly alien to Father Dolphus. They took up the topic of the wealthiest burghers of Denkendorf—the Uffenbachs, the Häckels, the Texlors, and even the Lingens, and none of them came off better than the others. Master Fröschlin was in his element. He provided ample proof that behind his unsightly exterior he possessed all requisite characteristics necessary for any respectable and influential burgher: he was an excellent conversationalist, he had an opinion on every topic, and he was never at a loss for amusing maliciousness as well. He therefore had every hope that he might be asked to fill the position of monastery physician. I myself began to believe in this possibility when I saw that as the conversation turned serious, the two men became so gentle with each other that I practically had the impression they had fallen in love. The tongue of Master Fröschlin was loosened; I had never seen him like this before. Inasmuch as I could understand his words, they were true gems. "We are in need of the greatest discernment," he said, answering one of the prior's questions, "in order to read the past as the present. Just as in the elementary schools the New Testament always begins with the Gospel according to Saint John, so do we regard historians as the most facile of writers. For can we know the past if we do not understand the present? And who could hope to create a correct notion of the present without knowing the future—for it is the future that determines the present, and thus the past, just as it is intention that determines an instrument's nature and use." Here Father Dolphus interrupted, and for the first time I discovered a wrinkle on his forehead. "Master Fröschlin, do you mean to say that the theologians, just like the scholars of the past, turn every moment on its head without having gained the least knowledge from it?" "Yes, of course," Master Fröschlin answered readily and unsuspectingly, and if he himself had read this moment from the future as he wished, he would have suspected that he now rushed to his own doom. "The scholars of history and the theologians, for the most part, are simply such people"—he continued underneath the ever more piercing gaze emanating from the cardinal's portrait—"who read one page daily from the *Etymologicum magnum,* noting down perhaps three or four words." Master Fröschlin continued that he regarded anatomy as a kind of key, and so did not seek the art of life amid the arid skeletons of history of which only the prophet can foretell if veins and blood shall grow upon them and whether they shall be covered by skin. For there is no life within them—only if the prophet shall utter his prophecies to the wind.

Master Fröschlin was in an excellent mood, and as we stepped out the monastery gates he even noted that surely we would be passing through these gates on many more occasions. I did not share his enthusiasm; still, it was as much of a surprise to me as to my master when on the following day a boy arrived from the monastery's boarding halls returning the gift which I had taken to Father Dolphus on my first visit. On the holy rood, carved out of one piece of wood—I was seeing this cross for the first time—the body of Christ did not face outward, he did not face those standing around the cross who, according to Luke, simply stared and who, according to Mark, cursed Jesus, saying, Thou that buildest the temple in three days, come down from the cross—instead, his body was turned inward, almost sinking halfway into the cross, as if he wished to draw back, to disappear once and for all into it, from which now only the back of his neck, shoulders, back, and the upper part of his thighs were thrown into relief, and, most sharply, his heels.

The boy who brought back the holy rood had no message from the prior.

"Are you looking at his heels, Johann?" Master Fröschlin asked me.

The heels of Jesus Christ were unnaturally sharp and large, just as when the prow of a sinking ship suddenly grows larger, or the nose protrudes from a dying man's face, emaciated to skin and bones. I could not fathom what this meant.

All I could see was that the cheer had disappeared from the face of Master Fröschlin; he lost his appetite, and frequently bickered with Mistress Agnete. His affection for me was unchanged, and he spent perhaps even more time with me than before. Therefore I was truly ashamed to find his ugliness—which until then had struck me as a kind of pleasant joke—ever more repulsive, and I fear it could be read from my countenance.

One day I came to him with the idea that I would go to the monastery and speak with Father Dolphus. Master Fröschlin made no answer, pretending not to have heard me. What I would say to Father Dolphus, or what I would ask him for, I myself had no idea. Once again I walked along the same path as two months earlier, once again I stood beneath the two tall oak trees. I knocked at the winged gates with the ram-headed knocker. I heard no noise from within. Once again I was about to reach for the ram's head, when I suddenly heard a tired shuffling and the key rattling in the door.

The prior's housekeeper opened the gate like someone who had been woken up from a dream, although it was already afternoon. She asked what I wanted. I told her I wished to speak with the prior. With that she turned on her heel, then returned after a short while and said that the prior was not receiving. In my foolishness, I insisted, assuring her that I would not take undue advantage of Father Dolphus's patience: I wished to pose him but one question. The housekeeper once again left and returned, more quickly this time, with a message from the prior: neither I nor my master should ever trouble him again.

That evening, Master Fröschlin informed me that there was no point to my remaining in his house: as far as he could tell, he had already instructed me in all that he knew; from this point on I would only be a burden to him. From his outstanding collection of maps he took one and, handing it to me, enjoined me to set off the next day at an early hour, while the city was still asleep, and to subsequently avoid Denkendorf as well as the surrounding area.

This latter promise was easy to make, as returning to the abandoned theaters of my life is not something I favor. As to the fates of poor Master Fröschlin and Mistress Agnete after my departure, I do not know, although years later I heard that unknown persons broke into their house one night at Christmas and smashed their heads in with a hatchet. I hope this is not true. I did hear, however, about Father Dolphus that when the next war broke out, he supplied wood to the French from the monastery forest until the side of the hill was completely razed, drawing upon himself the intense wrath of the denizens of Denkendorf. Surely this, and of course the lack of wood, were the reasons why the prior was buried without a coffin, his face turned toward the ground, in front of the monastery gates between the two tall oak trees. The grave was marked with a cross made of two oak branches tied together. And for many years afterward, no one sat in the prior's seat. It seemed that the bishop did not consider the matter of choosing a successor as urgent. The war raged on, everything the residents of Denkendorf possessed had been requisitioned, and yet even this did not protect them from the incursions of the French.

5

In the Garb of Babel

The next day at dawn, with the map and some under-clothes in my sack, I set off without casting even a glance back at the monastery rising above the city or at the two oak trees. I did not bid farewell to little Elsie, the daughter of the baker Johannes Seeliger, who during my time in Den-kendorf had gifted me with many pleasant hours. I took with me the fragrance of fresh loaves, of her pinafore, of her red hair unraveling extravagantly below her neck from beneath the stitching of her bonnet, and of her flour-white freck-led skin, and if I didn't take it very far, I took it at least to Lindau, where my nose was struck by other smells—those of horses and gunpowder: I joined the calvary regiment of Count Frangipan, which had been founded in Bavaria, then, after the death of the Bavarian Kaiser, was admitted to ser-vice in the Netherlands. He had no need for a feldsher, and yet they took me en suite; in addition the regiment paid for my horse's provisions, and thus I was able to put aside a tri-fling sum.

From this day on, I devoted my life to the games of war. I took part in many atrocities and horrors and, of course, much amusement as well. My attention was ceaselessly en-gaged, and I did not want for more ironically inclined ad-ventures, requiring all my imaginative faculties to remain present to that which inundated and revolved—in a word, happened—all around me; and yet if I think back on it, I recall only the incessant boredom, yes, and the emptiness: at times charging off toward something, at other times replete with slowly trickling events, and yet in its entirety unmovable; most peculiar of all was how this boredom formed the sediment of those days and hours when my life was truly in danger. The weather, of course, did not renounce its customary delights. It thrust sudden storms and abundant rains down upon us, immersing men and horses up to their knees in sticky mud; at other times it ravaged the fields with fire, so that there was nothing to bake with, neither barley nor millet. And yet these astounding capers brought no change whatsoever either to the endless marches commencing in earliest spring, enduring until the first frost in the fall, or to the peace and quiet lasting from November until winter's passing. We had two seasons, and from one year to the next they differed from each other in no respect. No matter whether a man wore a red or white uniform: in the aimless struggle of strength and resistance he was a worthless speck of dust. In the first days, however, it was not the immutability of the years that we experienced, but the whirling and inundation of the days. Nothing but waiting, nothing but commotion. How strange then, that from this time, my memory hardly preserves anything but a few flashing pictures which, just as quickly, fade away:

In Brussels, the monastery of Our Lady: the wounded—writhing, hacked into pieces—are being brought in. I observe their tortures coolly, I take almost no notice of them.

The jumbled mass of chariots and transport coaches stranded by the side of the road while trying to escape from the city. The men amuse themselves by shooting at the boundary stones, the bullets ricocheting back, whizzing above our heads.

In the town of Charles le Roy, on the rue de Croisement, a horse slips and falls down in broad daylight; it cannot get up again. Blood gushes from its knee. I turn my gaze away; I sense a grimace spreading across my face.

The haste of a young soldier as he steps out of a brothel. I cannot get out of the way in time and bump into him; like two balls knocking against each other, we both recoil. The soldier says something and hurries on. I don't know why my eyes chose precisely his face to chisel into my memory. And yet here he remains before me with his sharply cut nose, his smooth blond hair, his strong chin, and his clear, almost childish gaze. What became of this soldier? He probably remained there at Bergen, near Brussels, or someplace else. He'd been rushing to rake in something quickly from the manly joys; he didn't have much time.

A dark hillside, scattered with prickly blackthorn and thick elderberry bushes: French soldiers are hiding behind them. Our soldiers run toward them from behind the ridge; they are weightless, as if somebody were dreaming them—but the dreamer has clearly miscalculated. The assault should not have occurred like this. The soldiers who get within a stone's throw of the bushes come to a dead halt and look back: they see that most of the troop has remained behind. And suddenly more of them are falling down. Their falling is weightless, like that of puppets. Chaos breaks out, despair. Now the soldiers approaching from the bottom of the ridge are also beginning to fall. A Prussian major—he had been watching the battle with us—steps out. He walks into the empty space, and placing two fingers in his mouth he whistles, as to a dog. At this sign, his squadron marches out. They are young mute soldiers in dark Prussian uniforms. They slowly proceed before us, their steps rapid, one or the other glancing at us. This victorious death march is uplifting and beautiful.

Pictures, pictures. Within them is the nothingness of time, that which in the depths of every aberration remains unchanged. In comparison to them, how loquacious are the stories, the eternal confusion of the world! And yet, if I think well upon it, I enjoyed this confusion; my own garb of Babel never lost its native hues. He who goes about in the garb of Babel should not be surprised that his ambiguities are not understood by the others. And as my thinking was dominated by scatteredness, my speech by derisive reasoning, and my behavior by impudence, I myself can hardly wonder that in Ghent, in Flanders, I was accused of espionage. For a moment, I was even tempted by the idea of not protesting against this charge. But the second lieutenant, in front of whom I was dragged, did not appear to be much given to humor; I feared being thrashed within an inch of my life if it emerged that I was not a spy. In other words, the true task of any spy is nothing more nor less than to prattle on according to his own liking, finally promising to deliver the news, from now on, in the opposite direction for good pay. Most of the spies operational at that time were serving both the French and the Germans; everyone knew this. For spies live in the stories, they are the only ones for whom time is more than nothing, and as they are the good companions of the creations of imagination and memory, helping them to reconquer the world, and no one would chase them away. Therefore anyone who has even a drop of common sense will begin to spy of his own accord, without being asked to do so; to wit, such a person will cram empty time full of stories, the more unlikely and incredible the better. Such a person will fabricate the world, which God only created: He did not make it up because He did not know death, and He did not know time. Such a person will fabricate the secrets of others, secrets as yet unborn in their heads. And if, after all this, someone accuses him of being a spy, if he isn't a complete fool he will receive the accusation like a royal medal of honor pinned by the king himself upon his chest. But I was an idiot, and so I tried to protect myself and did not even realize that by doing this I was materially contributing to my own beating. Namely, the lieutenant who interrogated me, as he sucked on his rotten tooth, clearly enjoying the taste of the moisture he extracted from there, might have reasoned in the following way: The question is not whether the person who stands before us is telling the truth or if he is lying but whether we shall be gullible or suspicious. And if we are already posing this question, we need only decide the form our suspicion should take. For many are the ways of suspicion, but during interrogation there is only one: the twisting of the fingers, the thumbscrew. Let us start from the assumption that the person before us is lying: we will have him thoroughly beaten by men who know their trade well. The chief characteristic of a thorough beating is not that it be bloody, although it may well be that, but that it know the nature of fear and freedom. For only he who hoards the remnants of his freedom is capable of fear; he has not yet forgotten the future, even if in his current wretched state he can only hope the future might show up in ripped and bloody clothes. Whoever is afraid can never fully part with his beautiful memories; his body, soon to be covered with wounds, has not yet become the pilgrim of a deserted wilderness. Therefore let only patient and melancholy men become interrogators. Because what happens if we have someone beaten—remember, it always starts with a few blows—someone against whom we can make the most absurd accusations, or the most banal, as is the charge of espionage? Well, if he is still capable of fear, the thumbscrew will make him defiant like yeast being dripped into lukewarm milk, only serving to embolden his self-awareness, and if he has been lying until now, we can be certain that he will be lying even more from this point on. To become angry at this is foolish. With no rage, and no emotion, we could even say, with cool rationality, we increase the pressure of the screw, the target of which might be the kidneys or the cardia. As for the words of the accused, we shall for the time being not pay any attention to them, not even if we observe that he has collapsed from the blows, from the pain, because collapse is nothing more nor less than the ultimate confusion of truth and lies. And, of course, of freedom. Because whoever has spoken the truth, who has confessed, for example, that he is not a spy, and in truth he is not that, shall in a moment try to satisfy our demands, and although he is still wavering, internally he has already accepted his guilt, and he is, within certain boundaries, ready to cooperate with us against his own self, if only to avoid further blows. But we may not be satisfied with this. We are obliged to increase his tortures even further, for his own good, so that he may finally become himself, and if we lag behind the limit of his threshold of pain by a single blow or ripped-out fingernail, we may glimpse that person as he plunges, broken, into his own genuine existence, finally beyond all hope and all fear. Truth opens up like a yawning, empty abyss beneath him. What he is saying now, as he whispers, cries out in pain, groans, is no longer meant for us and not even meant for himself, but for that yawning abyss from which no future can be hoped, and in which everything that he believed to be his own past is lost—and thus we can be certain that truth is pain which surpasses all endurance.

That is what the French lieutenant might have been thinking. But even if he had been thinking otherwise, he still bequeathed me with the greatest thrashing of my own life in Ghent, and with complete futility, as in the end my protestations of the beginning—that I truly was not a spy—were borne out. Assuming that a spy is the one who acquires the secrets of others. And what of the unhappy man who has no idea of what a secret is and consequently is unaware that with every other sentence he betrays a secret? If he just speaks and speaks like someone who covers the table with all kinds of foods, so that he does not have to serve up true delicacies? Because the greatest secret of all has concealed itself for all eternity, and nothing can ever be spoken of it.

That is why we are free; surely, this is the single fount of freedom.

I abundantly practiced my freedom, and the joys of speech as well, when, accompanying the regiment of the Swiss general, von Diesbach—it was now one year later, and I was on the French side—I visited Brussels for the second time, mournfully, because the war had stripped the larders of the city and its environs of all provisions. And all I did was talk, just talk. Everyone knows something, therefore what anyone might have to say is inexhaustible if you include the repetitions. I spoke of my studies, I spoke of the healing arts, that wretched handiwork which obliges a person to fuss and toil over something in the Jewish manner, or possess the glib tongue of a market woman selling kale, so as to conceal, as a professed and faithful disciple of both the senses and matter, that the laurel wreaths of his intellect were bestowed upon him from the great Hippocrates to the executioner's hand today. For was it not Master Fröschlin who taught me that whoever has not filled a cemetery with corpses is not a physician? And if this is the case, can there be any greater physician than war? For surely the greatest affliction—let us admit—to weigh upon human beings is not that we must die amid pain but that we must, until that point, fill our lives with something. In the end fifty, sixty, or seventy years is a long time. And if we cannot think of anything better, war, as a remedy against all kinds of boredom, is hardly the worst thing with which to fill up a life. Do not the greatest writers, from Homer to today, provide evidence of this, those writers who tell us stories about nothing other—and in the least boring way possible—than wars and wars? In short, war is a good physician, because if it does not heal trouble, at least it shortens it. And so in this way, I made my argumentations, and I reaped the laurels of laughter as well in giving a good drubbing to the philosophy of our time, for it is barely a philosophy, and yet it wishes to make us believe that we shall soon be taking our nightstands with us into the trenches, where we shall be sipping lemonade and other refreshments, and if we must shoot at each other, we shall do so with perfumed gunpowder.

The consumption of a great deal of hard spirits had already undermined the facility of my audience's taste, which state I can also thank their being easily enthralled by such foolishness. Or at least for a certain time, because in the spring of 1746 first the bread ran out all at once, when the Bavarians plundered three of our carts in a surprise attack, then our brandy—with which we had been relieving the pain of our defeat—ran out, and finally there was no more beer, which we drank simply to quench our thirst. But General von Diesbach knew that a soldier, no matter what the circumstances, must fill his belly, otherwise in no time he will turn into a wild beast. In any event, the general, on rare occasions, would mutter to himself, although we still heard from him several times a day that the hero's true cosmetic was the sweat dripping down his brow. And when he saw that with the ebbing of our reserves, exasperation, ready to explode even without cause, was painting ever more frightful contours on the soldiers' faces, he decided to give me part of my soldier's pay in French thalers to convert to Netherlandish money and purchase bread and ham wherever I could. I can thank my knowledge of languages for this task having fallen on my shoulders—well, and of course the fact that when the general looked around, I appeared to be the only one in the immediate vicinity still possessed of a sound mind. And what this "sound mind" meant in my case will soon emerge. I gathered up all my belongings and that very hour set off for Sint-Niklaas, where I could hope for full baskets while my regiment marched on from Cauwerburg along the banks of the river Schelde. My sack filled up nicely, and I was not saddened when I realized that I would not be able to catch up with the hungry regiment of General von Diesbach: the Bavarians were occupying every area they left behind. In addition, the sack was heavy, and there was no way for me to make lugging it around more comfortable, its burden weighing heavily on my shoulders. For these reasons, and, well, as I had been incessantly hungry ever since I'd joined up under the command of Count Frangipan, I judged that the time had come to lighten my burden. I sliced off a good-sized piece from the ham and the bread, and by the banks of the river, at the base of a willow tree, I gave myself over to tranquil contemplation. Here the bank of the river Schelde turned into a thickly overgrown marsh, and as we were already past the spring rains, in places it broadened out nearly into a lake, creating a number of small islands. Geese, cranes, all kinds of ducks and woodcocks as well as multitudes of birds unknown to me flocked in that place, where—failing to keep in mind the virtue of moderation—I crammed my stomach full with ham until it nearly burst; the meat's tasty, salty liquid was particularly agreeable. The effect, in such quantities, was similar to that of the poppyseed: I slept deeply, assaulted by feverish hallucinations. My intestines sounded the awakening bugle. Perhaps the ham was rotten, or some faulty ingredient might have slipped into the marinade; in any event, I was assaulted by painful stomach cramps and soon drenched in sweat. Well, so finally upon me lay the cosmetic of the hero! I ripped off myself the treasurer's trousers, tearing off a great burdock leaf, and crouched behind a bush. Hardly had I finished my business and reached for the leaf to wipe my backside clean when I heard German words being spoken. If my trousers had not been rolled down around my ankles, perhaps I would have considered a course of action, but I had no other choice than to conceal myself motionlessly in the bush, praying to the sparrows not to betray my presence. My compatriots soon pulled me out of the bush, along with my sack, laughing. So once again I fell prisoner, this time to the Habsburg Imperial Calvary Regiment of the Kalnocky Hussars, and I can state that they had the same thing on their minds as the French. They too saw me as a spy, but their perseverance was not equal to that of the French. After a few blows and pummels, it was enough, in order to expel the last trace of suspicion from myself, to merely enumerate the names of the officers serving in the cavalry regiment of Count Frangipan.

But what is the shadow of suspicion compared to that of death? Suspicion keeps asking, Who is this person?—and no response will ever satisfy its curiosity. That is precisely why there is no need to worry about these questions: just be ready, until your last day, to give an answer—lie, make mistakes, because you could never tell enough lies or be so mistaken that your words would not yet contain a grain of credible truth. The shadow of suspicion is therefore your own self: it is what is told about you on the wall of the cave as someone holds a candle in front of your face, or, in a later age, a hundred-watt lightbulb. Death has no need of instruments of interrogation, if only because not even a spark of curiosity has ever gotten caught in it. For death, all that matters is that you exist, that you take up some space in this world, but as to what fills up that space, death is not concerned. It is enough for death that you are preoccupied with it, that from the light of your own life you lend it an ominous cast; now it can threaten you with your own shadow, as with the most dreadful of phenomena. But calm down, because death only wants an audience. It is therefore advisable to observe its blustering shadow play with a bored expression: then the figure of the dauntless Baron Munchausen will be nothing more than an impoverished playwright.

This is what I did as well when, amidst the booming of the cannons, the knife slipped in my hand and I severed a vein whose bleeding I was unable to stop, or when, after a wretchedly botched amputation, the patient, still writhing, slipped out of my hands, although it would have been better for him to die than for the remainder of his life become as the dust of the street. And I never would have been able to saw through and patch up all those battered skulls if I had not regarded them as so many empty walnut shells, because we will not name that soft moist mass—so much like the kernel of the walnut when its golden-brown membrane is peeled away—as any kind of content. But no matter what kind of bored expression I cut, it would have been a shame for me to deny that in a few respects I did bear a resemblance to Baron Munchausen, about whom Rudolf Erich Raspe, the outstanding scholar, notes somewhere that he would pretend to believe the lies of this or that impertinent character out-bellowing the rest of the company, dulling its sober powers of discrimination; Baron Munchausen never disputed with such a fellow, never betrayed that he was well aware of the chattering false fictions, but after a few courteous remarks, he would direct the conversation to the subject of his own travels and adventures at war. And so in this way I too was the medicus of death, and I cannot say that the sight, splayed on the operating table of the battlefield, of legs slippery with blood, hands smashed to pieces, and bodies splattered with bone marrow horrified me; I even found much beauty there, just as everything is beautiful which has found peace, which has reached its goal. In the end death is just death; it is a mirror of neither the good nor the bad. And yet mirrors interested me, no less so than Baron Munchausen, even if for the most part I did not know what I saw within them. Otherwise I would not have bid farewell to Captain Morgenstern, whose calvary regiment I had joined as a feldsher after the Kalnockys had allowed me to take my leave, having furnished me with travel documents. Captain Morgenstern and I were quite fond of each other; I did not part from him even when the regiment was ordered to retreat to Borckel to stand sentry by the war-ravaged troops of the Saxon prince Hildburghausen. We didn't have too much to do, therefore we had time for friendship: the captain took me with him to The Hague in the winter of 1747, where we were billeted in the house of an Italian by the name of del Filato. Indeed, we were billeted so well that when the time came to return I decided the war could now reach its end in my absence; my share in its embroilments was complete.

And I can say that I never regretted my decision for a single moment. As to what sorts of tasks fell to me in the house of Signor del Filato, I shall not relate in this chapter: first we shall immerse ourselves in his darkened and empty gaze, as I used to do back then. My host looked upon the world with such dark and empty eyes—more precisely this darkness and emptiness prevented him from looking into the world, as if this darkness and emptiness had directly sprung from the eyes of Adam or Eve. Moses writes that when the eyes of them both were opened, it was as if a newborn piglet had opened its eyes; the man and his wife were so terrified by the light that they immediately put their hands in front of their own eyes, concealing themselves behind a large tree. God, however, thought that they were well placed there: I shall not call them forward, He thought, and I shall not heal their eyes, they shall not find Me, and they shall never call Me to them ever again.

I suspected that there was something similar in the emptiness of the gaze of Signor del Filato, a face that he had lost, a face so far away now, beyond every forest in the world, that it could never be brought back. As there is no heap of dreadfulness that imagination will not cast into its own light—as if we were always filled with sweet wine—I soon transformed my host within myself into the hero of various secretive romantic imbroglios, all the more because for as long as I resided in his house, apart from his daughter I never came across a single female person, if we do not count the evil-tongued Mistress Corn, who arrived from time to time to collect the laundry. For in The Hague, where the women were at once merchants, poets, generals, legislators, and good conversationalists, it was certainly impossible to accomplish any task without them.

These sorts of things are handled much better in France, I therefore commented one evening to Signor del Filato, but not because I had ever paid my respects in Calais or in Paris, moreover I certainly would never even have heard the name of Elisabeth Draper at that time: my intention was simply to loosen his tongue. I therefore related to him how one time, as I was strolling the streets of Calais and pondering my own luck to have come so far as the son of a poor woman, I glimpsed a lady stepping over to the door of a carriage. Having, on the first sight of the lady, settled the affair in my fancy "that she was of the better order of beings," I then laid it down as a second axiom, as indisputable as the first, that she was a widow, and wore a character of distress. Next to the carriage stood a young man, some kind of simpleton, who goggled at her in such an improper fashion that if his eyes had been hands the woman would have been obliged to slap him immediately. I straightaway resolved to action, for surely who would know better than I what it meant to be a widow. Respectfully, I requested the young man to introduce the lady to me. In this moment, even that trifling intelligence in his possession—it still somewhat loomed upon his face, like the lamp of a postal coach in the fog—died out, and he answered that he had not been presented himself. All the better, thought I. Turning toward the lady, I introduced myself, and taking on loan the name of a certain Monsieur Buisson, I inquired if she had come from Paris. No: she was going that route, she said. Well, I stated with some exaggeration, if not from Paris, then such a lovely lady as yourself could not reside anywhere but London. At this, a fine smile appeared on the lady's face, and perhaps she even blushed a bit, and she indicated with a slight motion of her head that she was not from London. Then Madame must have come from Flanders, I continued the game. From there, my lord, she answered. Oh, not from Arras? Or perhaps Cambray, or Ghent? Do not keep me in suspense any further, I entreated her. She answered, she came from Brussels. So, Brussels, I said. How could I have been so mistaken? That city is like a genuine hidden pearl among the false, and its ladies are not otherwise. Have you been there before, asked the lady, and I was indeed happy that already she turned to me with a question. Yes, Madame. I spent truly pleasant weeks there, I added, and as to what the illustrious sons of war there had wrought with the pleasanter sex, I kept my silence. I had the distinction, I told the lady, of being present during the cannonade of the city in the last war. She nodded her head slightly, and this movement convinced me once and for all that this widow of Brussels truly took me for a Frenchman. And this evoked in me what I had truly lived through during the siege of Brussels. When the German soldiers marched into the city, all the peasant boys from Pfalz and the striplings from Pomerania thought they were occupying the capital city of France. As they marched in dense rows, all along the streets and in the great squares, their wide faces, smiling, grew even wider, and, poking at each other again and again with their elbows, their rifles dangling, they repeated: Paris! Paris! And as I have always held error to be the sweeter sibling of hope, I had no intention whatsoever of dispelling the impression of the beautiful widow from Brussels (that is, I took her to be, for some reason, a widow), but the gaze of that simpleton bothered me, it nearly burned into my back, and already I feared that because of him I would ruin my role.

I tried to forget about him, and I related the siege of Brussels to the lady in exhaustive detail, portraying as well my own role, of course from the viewpoint of the French; I conveyed my inspiration at the defeat of the Kaiser and his army.

Still, I thought it more advisable to take my leave, thanking her for the conversation, because I was already convinced that the simpleton listening to everything behind my back had realized that as far as the second siege of Brussels went, at best I might have been the recipient of a few cannon shots myself, and that I was possibly not genuinely a Frenchman. The next day, however, in the rue de la Tomperie, a carriage stopped next to me; a woman's voice asked me to take a seat within. It was the widow from Brussels. She told me that of course she didn't believe even a scrap of what I had related yesterday in her presence, indeed she even doubted that my name was Buisson, but to tell the truth she was not curious about my name: she asked only that I accompany her on the road to Paris for as long as it pleased me to do so. The lady placed her hand upon my arm, and, in possession of all of her maturity, turned to me with such inimitable charm that I immediately forgot all sober considerations. As to what followed afterward, I assured Signor del Filato, the carriage shall remain silent. In Pontoise, I once again stepped out into the fresh air, and in a hostelry I consumed a leg of mutton with great relish.

My host laughed well upon hearing my story, as men tend to do upon hearing each other's boasts, but he did not repay my pains with a similar anecdote. I was on the point of losing all hope that I could loosen his tongue by relating my own tales when, a few days later, deep in thought and often pausing, he told his story to me. And as stories exist only for us to disseminate them, why should I conceal what I learned from Signor del Filato? I did not pry into what was and was not true in his words; similarly, I do not recommend you to do so, my dear reader: instead, I suggest that you give yourself over with no reservations—become the embodiment of what every story desires.

Signor del Filato was born in the city of Delft in 1708 on a Sunday in May. His father was Italian—from him he inherited his melodious surname, as well as a few Italian words. The nobleman Charles de Bier held my host underneath the baptismal waters in the church named after Saint Jerome, and gave him the name of Carlo, which had been the name of his father as well; in the language of his birthplace, however, he was referred to as Karel, if only because it was easier to pronounce. In his joking contrivances and banter, Karel far surpassed his siblings and companions; the concerns of all around him he took as trivial, having nothing to do with him. When my master drew on the whitewashed walls with charcoal, crimson, yellow earth, using whatever came to hand, sketching the likenesses of peasant boys and servant girls—one with a long, slanted, stumpy nose, another with an owl sitting upon his hunchbacked shoulders, and a third with crooked, club feet—no one suspected the alliance that had formed within him between resignation and artistic free spirit, and at such a young age. On a bitingly cold winter's morning, even before the sun had risen, he promised one of his father's servants that he would write a satirical ditty about a certain maiden who had spurned him if he would hold his tongue on an iron doorknob for as long as it would take him, Karel, to read the Lord's Prayer and a Hail Mary. The simpleminded lad took up the recommendation joyfully, savoring in advance his revenge, via poetic speech, for having been spurned. My host began to read; the lad's tongue was already frozen to the iron. The poor boy could not move from the spot, and when he tried to draw his tongue back, he cried out in his pain. Finally, he was able to break away, but he'd made a bad deal of it, because he had to leave a piece of his tongue on the doorknob.

Karel perpetrated yet another strange prank. All the children from the surrounding neighborhood, who liked to play with Karel because of his amusing ideas, had gathered round. There was one among them whose widowed mother had had tailored for him a new white linen coat, and on that day he was wearing it for the first time. The boy strutted in front of Karel, who duly praised the boy's new outfit. And as just then the wild cherries were ripening, Karel alerted the boy that the tailor had forgotten to hem the coat, but if he would stand still for a moment, he would be glad to fix this. The boy consented, and Karel set to work. With the squeezed-out juice of the wild cherries, he drew a double hem on the coat, then to the side, and the front, and in the back, not forgetting the sleeves, on which he drew some flamboyant butterflies. The boy believed that he was now greatly smartened up; his appearance would delight everyone. His conceit could have ended badly if Karel had not outwitted the trouble to come. Realizing that as soon as his mama saw the "trimming" on the boy's coat, she would beat his bottom, Karel promised the boy a handful of wild cherries if he would allow him to paint something on his backside. After much reluctance, the boy turned his bare bottom toward the sun so that the painting would dry quickly. With great gusto, Karel painted a grimacing devil's face. When it was dry, the boy enthusiastically ran home to show his mother how beautifully his clothes were decorated. The lady, just as Karel had expected, was seized by infinite rage, and grabbed a cane to thrash her son. But as soon as she pulled down his trousers, with a shriek of "Virgin Mary, Saint Joseph!" she collapsed, fainting. Upon hearing her cry, the neighbors ran over, the boy managed to escape the beating, and when the affair came to light, everyone laughed heartily at the prank.

My host was slowly growing older, but he never left off his various tricks. He made drawings of strange figures with disjointed limbs at home on writing paper and on the walls in the streets. When his parents and relatives realized what an original and lively spirit resided in the boy, they sent him to a suitable painting master. Under Lucas de Born, Karel greatly developed in painting, and yet his father took him away from that atelier. His second, and final, painting master was Peter Cottem; he resided for a long time in his Kortrijk residence. Master Cottem was proficient not only in painting but in writing, although his mode of thinking was a little old-fashioned. From his hands emerged magnificent textbooks, even, for example, about Noah. He studied how the ark might have been built, he showed, in theatrical works, how Noah gave his sermon to the people about the Flood, how the animals were gathered together, how they filed into the ark, how the raven and the dove were released, and how, after they left the ark, a sacrifice was made before God. All this was presented en scène very pleasingly and artistically; numerous personages made their appearance. On a fairly large sail canvas he drew the corpses of many people and animals as they tossed about in the water. This piece of canvas was hoisted onto the stage, and with hand pumps, water was sprayed onto a house on the stage: so much water came pouring down that one could have easily thought it a downpour, the result of which, however, was that the multitude of viewers, who had flowed here from the nearby cities and villages to watch the performance, were obliged to draw farther back, and to wonder in amazement at where this vast quantity of water had come from. The old people, with pity in their hearts, lamented the dead, and they also deeply felt the fear of the living, because the view in front of them showed the ark tossed about on the waves.

At the time that I came to know Signor del Filato, he too had composed a theatrical piece about Noah. Except in this drama, Noah was already a drunken old man. In the tavern, he would go on and on about the Flood to anyone at all, describing how he had carpentered a zoo-sized ark, but the most important thing was for good old Noah, this clown from before the Flood, to be remunerated in the form of a stein of barley beer, or even better, two. One day, however, God came to visit him again. Noah recognized Him immediately, although he remembered His face as younger, but then why wouldn't God get old like anyone else? God asked Noah what had happened to the ark made out of cedarwood. And Noah answered that the cedar had been needed for firewood. God asked Noah where were his sons, as strong as cedar trees. And Noah answered that both of them were well set up, they had become wealthy, and neither of them bothered with him anymore. And then God grew sad. He thought that He had gotten nowhere with this Flood of His, people were not serving Him, they didn't even bother with Him, and He hardly ever even came across a friendly soul, someone who could understand Him, apart from this old drunkard. So they sat there in the tavern until closing time like two old veterans. They talked about the old days, either with longing or rage, all those wretched swindlers who tried to save their own skin, and how, when they saw it wasn't working, they begged for at least another year or two, another month or two, and their weeping and moaning when they finally understood there was no mercy. When the tavern closed, the innkeeper shoved them out into the street. "You old scoundrels, you've had enough to drink today!" The innkeeper was the last one who saw the face of God in this world. Foolish old man! He disappeared, and Noah disappeared with Him as well, Noah took God to himself, so that at least he would have someone to talk to.

This was a rather bitter story, but Signor del Filato had had his joyful days as well. His happiness was otherwise known as Véronique, who was the daughter of Master Cottem. My host painted her countless times as she laundered clothes, cleaned fish, sewed in front of the window, or wrote letters by the large oak table where her father usually sat. Véronique's fragrance permeated the room. It was clear that heaven had predestined them for each other. Master Cottem had Signor del Filato sit down next to him as if he were his own son, serving him with a large piece of dill-spiced fish. Only that tranquillity slowly but surely dulled the lovers' feelings. It was enough for Signor del Filato to have more than the usual amount of work or, on the contrary, for Master Cottem to fall short in orders, or for the sunlight to fail to unwrap the sky from its autumn clouds for weeks on end; dry certainty crept, imperceptibly, into the place of excitement and doubt. But it was already too late for them to reconsider. My host remained with Master Cottem, not too long afterward taking Véronique as his wife. He finished up the canvases for the most part now, also completing independent assignments. Master Cottem worked exclusively on commission, painting portraits, landscapes, and everyday, idyllic scenes for the guilds and well-to-do burghers, and almost unnoticeably—albeit for the watchful eye unambiguously—the traits of Véronique appeared in every single picture. The inclination of the hills recalled the arc of her forehead, the bends in the rivers evoked her melancholy smile, and in the matrons' severe gazes there was something of Véronique's warmth, which so quickly clouded over. The colors of Karel's pictures, however, grew ever darker. He and Véronique were sorry for each other, and they were often silent.

Then one winter day everything changed. Véronique was expecting a child. Signor del Filato, who truly was entranced by the thought of his prospective fatherhood, immediately envisioned a small assistant at his side to whom he would show, step by step, how to work with colors, with the models, and who soon would become a true master, his work sought after by those in distant countries. For the time being, the only sign of this inner transformation was that Signor del Filato suddenly became attentive and considerate. "No need to be so protective, I'm not made of alabaster," Véronique kept saying. When her time came, my host ran for the midwife, who, palpating her stomach, foretold a difficult birth. Yet that didn't happen. Carla, after a few hours of labor, was born safe and sound and healthy. Véronique, however, never rose from her bed again. Within two weeks, the fever swept her away.

From this time on, Signor del Filato became a recluse. Only the wet nurse was allowed into the house. A few weeks later, the nurse called his attention to the fact that when someone moved a finger in front of little Carlita's face, she did not follow the movement with her eyes. Signor del Filato answered that it would be a miracle if Carlita could already sense movement in front of her eyes. After this, the wet nurse no longer mentioned her observations. But a suspicion had crept into my host's thoughts. When he was alone with the little girl, he made more and more attempts with both larger and smaller objects, which he drew slowly across Carlita's face, sometimes very close, sometimes farther away. His attempts always continued until Carlita's eye moved in the desired direction, and if he waited for this in vain, then he reassured himself with the thought that Carlita was sleepy. Still, he could not lull himself for long. Even if he did not say so out loud, he knew that Carlita was blind.

Signor del Filato then put down his brush, gave away the canvases, and burned his sketches and charcoal drawings. Even so, he did not become a sullen man. In Carlita's blind gaze, in her every movement, Véronique was present, unchanging, albeit distantly, because her behavior, her loudness, her scatterbrained character differed so much from her mother's sympathetic reticence that any resemblance between them existed only in the eyes of my host. Eyes that Carlita herself had no need of to make her way around the house and outside the house, and not even there, but by the nearby dike as well, around the mill—in a word, everywhere. Signor del Filato never sought any explanation for this ability of his daughter's; neither did others. Anyone who did not know that Carlita had been living in darkness since birth and saw her gathering vegetables from the ditch or pouring out water for the dog would think her to be like any other little girl. But anyone who spoke with her immediately became confused. Some said that a blinding wildness was reflected in Carlita's eyes; others said that it was defenselessness and pain. I myself saw Carlita's eyes as everything but not as a mirror. Her eyes were like a lake that swallows up light and from that light gives back nothing.

Signor del Filato did not reveal when and why they had moved from Kortrijk to The Hague, what his life was like with Carlita, or how it came to his mind to get married again; he related only one more incident, in which, if I think further upon it, I not only could have glimpsed the depths of the sadness of Signor del Filato, but could have also anticipated the events of the following weeks. It happened, in fact, that on a certain day Carlita disappeared from the house, leaving no sign for Signor del Filato as to where she had gone. The pitcher and the basket were both in their place. Neither was the bucket missing. Yet Signor del Filato was only truly filled with dread when he saw Carlita's bonnet on the top of the wooden chest, as Carlita never left the house without it. He ran to the neighbors, but he did not find Mistress Corn at home, only her son, who came out from the back of the house, from the stables, and hardly wanted to comprehend what was making Signor del Filato so anxious. And Peter Arend, the master blacksmith's assistant, had also not seen her; if he did not have work to do next to the anvil or the bellows, he usually stood outside in his leather apron by the workshop door, otherwise always left open, so no one could pass by without his noticing. Carlita, Peter Arend maintained, had not shown herself on Ship Hold Street, this tiny and out-of-the-way city stage, of which he'd been the constant observer ever since birth, so to speak. As to the mystery of how the street had gotten its name, by the way, neither he nor any other "indigenous resident" could give an answer. This part of the city gave no issue on to the sea, and for as long as anyone could remember, no one who had anything to do with shipping or boats had ever lived here: it was inhabited only by tradesmen, people so used to dry land that they grew dizzy even at the sight of the waves.

Signor del Filato searched in vain for Carlita all afternoon and night. No one had seen her, no one could direct him with any useful details. He felt that what happened was his fault, he accused himself of having left Carlita alone, and now he was afraid, as he searched for her, that he might be committing a fatal omission in every minute. At the time, in The Hague and in the surrounding cities, little boys and girls disappeared without a trace, never to be seen again. People were always speculating about what had happened to them—of course they suspected the soldiers, for in the end soldier folk, ever since the world has been the world, have always needed a kind of tranquillity which only girls and young women can provide, but of course no one knew anything for sure. There were some who believed the missing children had ended up at the bottom of the ocean, there were some who said they'd been taken to America. Thus, Signor del Filato, nearly losing his mind, ran along the streets, gazing into the gates of houses, examining squares, but he became disoriented and always ended up in places where he had already been two or three times before. He was nearly choking with fear. After all, Carlita was blind, and although she knew the surrounding streets well, she had never ventured farther away by herself, and it would be easy enough to do her harm. To consider that she might have strayed somewhere outside the city limits was dreadful. A Walloon regiment was making regular forays into the surrounding area. The news was that they had already attacked Rijswijk, plundering the houses, striking the men dead, even snatching away some of the womenfolk.

In his worry, Signor del Filato perceived that he was surrounded by an infinite number of signs: every object, every facade, every street corner, every gaze sent him a message telling him where to look for Carlita, but he didn't know how to read these signs, he didn't know this language being spoken by the curious faces turned toward him, the momentarily glimpsed city scenes, the residents busy with everyday activities, the objects in their infinite multitude, perhaps even his own haphazard decisions—which corner should he turn, whom should he ask if they had seen Carlita—yes, it was as if his own excited and fearful deviations were also speaking in this unknown tongue, and if he felt that he had understood this or that sign, if, feeling a strong compulsion to turn in this or that direction, he had run up and down many streets, then he always ended up right where he had started. Despite every calamity which had struck him in the course of his life hitherto, for the first time he was completely lost, and from this point on he was accompanied by a feeling, never to be fully extinguished, as if a stranger followed his every step from a hiding place, yes, a stranger who nearly hunted him, even if in his daily life he could still find some way to orient himself in this perplexing world.

He finally found Carlita beyond the city, amid the northern dunes. By that point, he was utterly exhausted. The series of shocks that had, ever since he had become aware of his daughter's disappearance, compelled him until now to cover a certain number of distances at random, as it were blindly, and ever more quickly—an inundation more audible than visible; and when it cast him upon the shore, he suddenly lost all his strength. Below, the bottom of the sandbars was partially overgrown by rustling clumps of heather, and Signor del Filato suddenly wanted to lie down, he had no more strength to remain upright; still he took one or two steps in the soft, moldering sands, and when he looked up at the moon looming dubiously, it was not he but rather his body that announced that the worry he had been feeling up till now about his daughter, because he really could not imagine what would happen if she died, had finally sunk into the darkness, into that darkness in which Carlita had always lived. The entire life of Signor del Filato as it had been ever since Véronique's death lay along the bottom of the spine of the sparsely vegetated, wind-rustled sands like an empty shell, a discarded snakeskin; his body—utterly worn out from the throbbing memories that belonged to no one now, to the invisible inundations—finally sank down.

The wind blew on his face; that was his last lucid experience.

In the morning, when he came to himself, every part of his body hurt. He felt that that decision which he had already made, or rather that had been made for him by someone else, had now once again been set aside, and yet there was not enough strength in him to find his place once again in the world which rumbled all around him, enclosing him. The sun was shining, he could hardly open his eyes. And when finally, he opened them again painfully, at the top of the sand dune, he glimpsed Carlita. She slept, deeply and peacefully.

6

The Report of a Pistol

The wall clock was brought in. My grandfather designated its place, right across from my bed. He hung it on a hook, ceremoniously opened its glazed door, gave the pendulum a push, and it began to swing back and forth. The small copper plate behind the glass was set in motion, and in the dark brown wooden casing of the clock, time began to pass. This, already, was my time. My task, though, was simply to observe. To observe as, in the evenings, my grandmother prepared everything she needed for baking bread: the flour, the yeast, the water and salt; to observe as she rolled up her sleeves, mixed the ingredients together, forcefully kneading the dough, pummeling it until water began to drip down from the eaves, until the sweat began to drip down from the small brooks above her eyebrows. Her movements were severe, dark, and serious. At such times, everything around my grandmother disappeared; she paid attention only to the dough. I liked to watch her because she did this from within, her entire body working, and yet at the same time everything, the apron-scented brown darkness, was completely still. When the dough was smooth and even, when it began to breathe, when it lived, my grandmother's disproportionately large lilac-colored hands began to slap the back of it, and, as if into swaddling clothes, she placed the dough in the trough, where, now covered with a kerchief, it rose during the evening hours.

The clock is already up on the wall, exactly opposite my bed, and so time has begun to pass for me: by the time it strikes four o'clock at dawn, by the time my grandmother slips out from underneath the eiderdown quilt and her bulky foot searches for her worn-out black shoes beneath the bed, by the time she takes the risen dough, now leavened and spongy, in the dough basket out to the summer kitchen to bake the bread in the stout brick oven, as well as the "gander's neck," the long curved strands of milk bread; by the time the bread and the gander's neck have been baked, I will be far, far away, impossible to reach. Gander's neck is a very delicious food. It's something like a Viennese pretzel, only larger and thicker. You have to wait until it dries out, then you slice it, pour boiling water on top, and sprinkle it with poppy seeds and curds. I've never eaten anything like it since.

Time has begun to pass, and now I cannot remember its taste. I have to leave immediately because I cannot tell everything to my grandmother. I cannot tell her that the previous day, a week before, or a month before, while she was out working in the potato fields and I set off to reach her on foot, along the road that was beginning to lead to nowhere, next to me a cart stopped. An old man sat on the driver's seat, or at least I saw him as being old; in reality he probably wasn't. He asked me where I was going. I told him, and even though I knew I wasn't allowed to get into the horse cart next to him, by the time I realized that, I was already being jolted along on the driver's seat. I didn't dare look at the old man, I stared at the hindquarters of the horse in front of me. Its hindquarters were good and strong, it moved at an easy pace, its hooves kicked up the dirt, and the cart had already left the village. Nobody passed us on the road, and we had to go around the mountainside to get to the fields. There was a dense fragrance of herbs, chamomile bloomed along the side of the road, and the hindquarters of the horse were steamy as they undulated. I tried to immerse myself in the fragrance, but my neck had grown completely stiff. Don't look over there, I kept saying to myself, don't look over there. The old peasant man suddenly grabbed my wrist. I didn't resist, I still didn't want to look. And he took my hand, took it to his trousers. I should have cried out for him to let me get down from the cart, but I had no voice. I touched his member. I didn't look at it, I didn't want to see. I am mute—soundless. And already the clock is rattling, already empty time is passing. I wait until they think I have fallen asleep. My uncle, who sleeps in the bed above me, is going to catch me, and say, "No, Bertuska! No!"—I have no idea how he can see from up there that I pick my nose. But I don't pick it anymore. I'm disgusted by my own hand. That grip has remained on it, the old peasant's hideous smell, I sense it, and although I should be able to cry out, I don't, and I know that what surrounds me now is finished for all time—I lie among the dead.

I go home to Ózd, but I don't find my mother and father there. My father worked in the mine again for a time after the war, but then a runaway mine cart smashed into his chest. Every bone was broken. Once again he ended up in the hospital, and although Miklós Horthy could not visit him this time with an iron cross medal as in 1943, and Mátyás Rákosi had absolutely no intention of visiting hospitals to pin red stars on the patients' chests, my father still recovered; once again he became a policeman. During the war he had worked as a policeman for only one year. Toward the end of 1944, at the time of the general mobilization and despite his wounds, he was called up as a soldier, and a few days later he was sent to Germany to dig anti-tank ditches. His ditches did not impede any tanks. They roared on toward the river Elbe, and he stood there in Hamburg at the mouth of the Elbe; he stood there emaciated and filthy, he looked into the distance and wondered if he should get on a boat, leaving everything behind, and sail to America like his companions. The sea is the greatest of temptresses. Distance, the thought of a different life—these are more enticing than the most beautiful of women. My father came home, though. He came home, but not by a direct route. Near Hannover he was taken in by a peasant woman. He worked at her house for weeks, and the German woman, who had lost her husband on the Eastern Front, didn't want to let him go. It can be imagined how happy my mother was to hear this story. In her view, the entire war had been invented only to vex her: my father was dawdling somewhere in Germany, who even knew who he was getting cozy with while she struggled with me here at home. I was a weepy child with frequent stomachaches, she couldn't put me down even for a minute. In the air raid shelter she had to keep the light on so I could go to sleep, my mother never knew if it was day or night, her eyes would begin to close, and she'd be woken up by the flashlight falling on my head. Then, in the winter of 1945, my father somehow turned up at home. He showed her his right forearm: at some point after he'd been in Hannover, he'd had my mother's name tattooed inside a heart above his wrist. And he showed her the map stamped with the eagle of the Third Reich he'd gotten in Hamburg. He was proud of that, not only because the Third Reich was, after all, a serious matter, but because the eagle and the swastika for him symbolized his own freedom: the one who is free is the one who can live a different life from the one he has been living until now; he isn't completely there where we glimpse him, even if, for example, he has covered a thousand kilometers on foot to arrive at the place he will later yearn to leave. You can never be in just one place, do you hear, from now on you will always be in two places, from this point on you will always be with two women—"Kannst du es begreifen," the German woman said to him, "du kannst weg, bleibst jedoch hier, denn alles geschieht gleichzeitig." It was as if the eye of the eagle of the Third Reich had found its prey.

But simultaneity, perhaps, is merely a deception of desires, a lie that lives in the trousers of a man. Rather than wanting to see clearly in this matter of desires, rather than presenting himself with pleasing lies—although who knows, perhaps deception is not the simultaneity of different lives after all—my father chose to complicate his life in a much more matter-of-fact and imagination-poor way, contenting himself with a single deception, which as a matter of fact was true, truer than I could ever judge: namely that he, in the end, was happy with my mother. And it was only on his deathbed that he dared think that perhaps he had not been happy with her, when at the end of a convoluted story he said that even a horse desires to be caressed sometimes. In any event, he put the map away into a drawer, taking it out only rarely, gazing at it as he sat with a glass of red-currant wine but doing so more to annoy my mother than anything else; even in his imagination, he planned no more murky adventures.

My mother had no respect for my father's privacy. For her, men were harsh, half-animal-like beings, and my father was no exception: with his excessively strong body, his sweat-soaked undershirts, his hairless, tattooed arms, his muddy, loin-smelling trousers, his wine slugging, and his rude cursing, he remained an illicit intruder into her more refined world, where, with every step, he bumped into yet another sign announcing a prohibition, forcing him to be ashamed of himself. But there was nothing she could do; the intruder was already inside the walls, already had his rights, and trotted around the house almost like a pig, dirtying the parlor with its muddy legs, dripping its moisture everywhere—and yet somehow my mother loved this intruder, she could not not love it, even as she assiduously struggled against it. This struggle slowly but surely withered within her the desire for a more refined life, from which finally nothing remained but a bitter sediment, a haughty, eternal dissatisfaction which in the course of the years accumulated in her to such an extent that in the end she could hardly catch her breath.

My father was first posted as a policeman to Szendrő, and then to Rudabánya. There were mountains, brooks and tunnels, ruts from horse-drawn cart wheels, sunken roads, and beneath the earth other invisible things as well. The dreams of ancient happy times slept in the earth: Rudi, the pre-historic man, and Gabi, his wife. There was still no deception; there were, however, weapons. One time Rudi put on an animal mask and smashed apart the skull of a man even more prehistoric than himself; he danced, and Gabi was proud of him. This was honest work, and there was nothing in it to be ashamed of. I love you, Rudi, you are big and strong. Rudi, however, wanted to be even bigger and stronger, big and strong enough to slaughter wolves and bears, to skin them, eat their flesh, then make a blanket from their hides and slip underneath that blanket with Gabi, because he liked nothing better than to snuggle up with Gabi by the fire. Thus painting the future in bright colors, Rudi set about carving knives. At first he carved them from bone, from hardwood and stone, then finally, when he had learned how to melt ore, he made blades out of metal. And so the knives became metal knives. Rudi was happy; now he danced all day because he was the strongest man around, and there was no animal that he could not take down. Only somehow things were not good with Gabi. What did this woman want? Why didn't she want to snuggle underneath the blanket with him? To cuddle together? To draw her finger along the side of his mouth? She was cooling off, turning away. When he thought about this, Rudi found that he had to drink the sap of the fermented fruit. To make a long story short, he was drinking more and more, until one day he plunged down, stunned, from a cliff, because down below he had caught a glimpse of another woman. Another woman, or perhaps a glimpse of Gabi as she was twenty years ago, when her face was slimmer, her gait more swaying, and her entire presence pure sunlight. Rudi asked the chasm who this woman was. Who is this woman, I don't recognize her? His body crooked into a question mark, a sorrowful question mark, because the woman was far away, and the chasm understood the sadness, it understood very well, and so the chasm yanked Rudi down into itself. Headfirst, he plunged, and his skull, in which newly formed hope had erupted into voluptuous foliage, was smashed apart. And the foliage of his imagination came to overgrow the entire mountain slope; centuries, or maybe even millennia, went by, until beneath the foliage, in the thick undergrowth covering the base of the tree trunks like pubic hair, somebody found Rudi's knife. He picked it up, examined it, and as he had a sense for perfection, beauty, and the good, the only adjustment he made was to close the blade back into the handle. And so the pocketknife was born, and thus equipped with the pocketknife, the men of Rudabánya became real men: beneath the foliage of their imaginations, magnificent women laughed at them, their eyes full of understanding. Among the women was Jolika from payroll, and Sacika, the young girl behind the counter in the agricultural collective grocery; her skin luminous and brown like the crust of freshly baked bread. And every evening, the true men of Rudabánya fought for the women of the foliage, stabbing their pocketknives directly into their opponents' abdomens, the blood flowing out in puddles in the dust; whether they were Gypsy or Hungarian it was the same color red. People who moved here from elsewhere asked, "What kind of people are these?" No one answered the question, just as no one answered most questions. In place of an answer, the police came along to separate the men fighting with their pocketknives; sometimes though, they came too late, and someone had already died.

Now, however, when it's Tuesday, and it's still only noon, the air barely moves in the village. My father, in his gray staff sergeant's uniform, freshly laundered (that's why it smells of gasoline) by my mother, can have his lunch in peace at the police station. Today he's having potatoes with paprika, into which, according to his habit, he dunks pieces of bread, and as he bolts down the potato slices, stabbed onto the tip of his fork with chunks of wiener sausage, the reddish pearls of grease stick to his mustache, the ornaments of lunch. There is no lack of anything. The confused chirping of the sparrows pours in through the opened window. Lunch can hardly be so peaceful when taken at the commander's desk, although in the village there momentarily is no need of a policeman; no one passes through the forest beneath the foliage of imagination. But just now someone is leaning his bicycle against the fence outside. It's the delegate from Ormosbánya, he's bringing a report again. He is a quarrelsome, officious man. The best thing would be to send him back to his mother's arse, but still it doesn't hurt to be careful with him. For the time being, my father can't decide whether he's being provocative or if he's just an idiot. Furthermore, he has a particular sense for picking the best times to stop by. My father has no wish for his lunch to be disturbed with a report. It can certainly wait. He knows all too well that the reports of the delegate from Ormosbánya—an agent of the State Protection Authority—are the kind that are not content to simply describe individual matters; instead, they are bills of indictment against authority in the face of its fading military might. We must not allow ourselves to slip into complacency, but continually develop our vigilance, we must not allow ourselves to be lulled, but continually maintain our state of military readiness, we must not disarm ourselves, but rearm ourselves, we must not demobilize, but mobilize, just as our enemies are doing. He must be a simple idiot, as opposed to a provocateur. It seems, though, that someone in the village is really arming himself, and with a more serious weapon than a pocketknife. The devil take him, this will certainly lead to some kind of police case! The spoon once again plows across the bottom of the saucepan, so that the least amount possible will be wasted of the thick, delicious gravy, and the last slice of cucumber as well disappears between the teeth.

Well, has this Antal gone mad? He's hiding a pistol? What does he need that for? And if he has a pistol, why is he showing it to people? He took it to Ormosbánya to get it repaired, as if he were taking a coat to the cleaners? My father, quickly wiping up the rest of the gravy from the bottom of the saucepan with a crust of bread, once again places the report from the delegate from Ormosbánya on the table before him. This will be hard to get out of, he thinks. From behind, three wise men with three sorrowful gazes are also leaning over the report. Two of them have abundant beards, the third is sparsely whiskered, his head almost completely bald. The three of them are sorrowful because, although the compassionate wisdom in their gazes never fully died out, in vain is their attention turned toward millions, in vain are they present, from Vladivostok to Weimar, in every police station, classroom, and courtroom; in vain do they know what the armies of police captains, teachers, pupils, judges, and mainly the armies of Party secretaries must do, as well as what they must think before acting—but they are tired already, they don't have enough strength to overcome all the foolishness, and yet people indeed can be formed, people are basically good. Yet the three of them are no longer capable of issuing clear instructions. You see, my father should be able to glean the right course of action from their eyes, or perhaps their tangled beards, if he's going to deal with them at all. But it doesn't occur to my father to ask them for advice; he sits with his back turned to the three portraits, which will be removed from the wall soon enough. Entangled as he is now in the contradictions of friendship and obligation, when there is no more gravy left to mop up in the small red saucepan, he certainly is in need of some advice, although he knows very well that no matter whom he asks the answer will be the same: "There is no friendship, no mercy! These are not the days for patting people on the head; they must be struck down without mercy!"

These, however, are not my father's words but those of the man with the balding pate and sparse beard on the wall. He's always saying things like that. My father isn't too happy to hear such words in general, and now not at all. Specifically, the teacher Antal Bokor, my father's friend, had a few days earlier inspected his old pistol which he'd kept ever since the war, along with some ammunition, and he established, with a distinctly felt pain over the passing of time, that this pistol didn't shoot anymore. Not that he was suddenly seized with the desire to shoot someone. Antal Bokor had had enough of shooting on the Russian Front. But if he could part from neither the pistol nor his memories, why couldn't he try to at least keep them in decent working order, as with everything else in his life as an exemplary old bachelor? So after the school day ended, he got on his bicycle and cycled over to Ormosbánya. A mechanic lived there who was good with pistols, and as it had been a long time since he'd held an item like this in his hands, he didn't try to disguise his excitement when he took the German Parabellum from Antal Bokor. He immediately disassembled the pistol to its components as if it were a clock, cleaned and oiled it, and filed some parts down, delighting in this truly wondrous piece of hardware:

that night it was ready to fire. But the mechanic was a man of the old school. He had no trust in any kind of ideology or theory, and even less in the notion of man's fundamental goodness, either generally or concretely; he had faith in his own work, in a task carried out honestly; already a rarity in these times. And a part of honest work must include evaluation. Since this was a pistol, he was obliged the next morning to nail up a target, prepared by his own hand, on the pigsty wall; he aimed at the center of the lower edge of the black circle. He hit the mark. When the trigger was pulled, the denunciation already lay on the desk of the police commissioner in Ormosbánya. The informer was, of course, the mechanic himself, who had similarly "recollected" many of his other clients to the police before.

Those three wise and sorrowful gazes have every reason to ensure that at this very moment, all the way from Vladivostok to Weimar, no staff sergeant's nape would be as sorrowfully scrutinized as was my father's, as mutely they practically cry out to him: "There is no friendship, no mercy!" And my father, as if hearing the silent cry, stands up, adjusts his jacket with his holster, and, stepping out of the garden gate of the station accompanied by a regular policeman, sets off along Kossuth Lajos Street, its foliage arching above, toward the school. There's no reason to hurry, of course. The school day hasn't ended yet; neither has his agony as to what to do next. And while he makes up his mind, we can peacefully return to his office in the police station and immerse ourselves in the aftermath, taking place years later, of this story, from which—as from a dream—the report of Antal Bokor's pistol shall startle us awake.

At that later time, the three of us, my father, my mother,

and I, lived in the police station's service residence—in what used to be the parlor, facing the street: the house differed from the others nearby only in having a separate, iron-grated entrance behind the porch; above it hung the police force shield with its red star. This emblem indicated that the house did not belong to the village but was the emissary of a distant power: if this power were not so distant that one could forget its existence for a single moment, it was yet distant enough that its own emissary hardly seemed to belong to it. In other words, we lived in a kind of no-man's-land, not only my father but my mother and myself as well—we both shrunk back from the gray uniforms filing past the window like shadows, from their pistols. Many times I observed that as my mother approached the small grocer's shop, the women standing there chatting would fall silent, or at least speak in much softer tones; the children with whom I wanted to play never invited me. I was sad about this but not too much; I told myself that their games would annoy me or frighten me to death. My mother too had to accept that in the village setting her identity was identical to that of my father even as she continued her silent and persistent struggle against him. And what else could she have chosen as a territory for struggle than my upbringing, where she could feel herself a priori to be victorious? Who even knows where she got the material to sew me ever more beautiful dresses, which then became the cause of my suffering as in these dresses I felt even more alien among the girls of the village, and yet I never would have exchanged my own pleated skirts and ribbons for their simple garments.

If I think about it, this part of my childhood was spent in the struggle of both shadows and clothes, a struggle revolving around my father, who, in the era of uniforms, flags, and marching, had been invested by two alternating state powers with the emblems of manliness and violence, such emblems as could only be gained from the hand of the state. For my father, his uniform admitted him into a better and more steadfast order. Early in the morning, he pulled on his policeman's jacket like a second skin, buttoning it up to the top before the mirror. Not only would this order have been disturbed if he had understood anything of my mother's frightening solitude, a solitude which she embroidered into the pillows, tatted into the finery of the lace, and sewed into my dresses, but the mere consciousness of the potential existence of any order, including one receiving him into its ranks, would have been disturbed as well.

Now, however, as my father in his gray staff sergeant's uniform walks toward the school along Kossuth Lajos Street with its foliage arching overhead in the company of a regular policeman, he suspects nothing of how the story will continue; moreover, he doesn't even know whether in a few minutes he will arrest his friend, the teacher Antal Bokor, or if some saving idea will occur to him; and so you, my dear reader, who have accompanied me this far, can easily step with me into that time when each of those beautiful shadows became like startled little dwarves who weren't even as tall as the windows of the one-story houses; they scurried on all fours lest anyone notice them. Of course, the three wise and sorrowful men could never have been mistaken. From Weimar to Vladivostok they had already seen enough wretched little dwarves by now. But all this wretchedness and dwarfishness filled them with so much pain and anger that they no longer had any strength: they themselves began to shrivel, at first down to the size of a hand, then they became stamp-sized. They were afflicted by an unknown illness. Their beards, hiding so many enigmas, fell out to the last hair. And as their strength resided in their beards, one morning, when already no one would have recognized them, the three Buddhist monks—for that's what they were by now—the great men of the revolutionary workers' movement, feeble and exhausted, slid down from the wall; now there were only three unadorned and faded spots to show they had ever been there, and nothing else. On the morning when my father noticed their absence, he became horribly frightened, and before all the assembled district, city, and county Party secretaries, their first and second deputies, the judges, teachers, and the organized youth from Weimar to Vladivostok could learn that the three bearded men were gone from the wall in Rudabánya and hold him, exclusively him, responsible—because the disappearance of these three heads could result in chaotic headlessness all the way from Weimar to Vladivostok—he urgently looked for three other portraits to cover up these faded spots; three portraits that could not cause any trouble according to any sober reckoning. In other words, at that time, in Hungary the portraits of the great men on the walls were being replaced.

As for such a portrait, which—scrutinizing it from every viewpoint and concluding that no trouble can emerge from its selection—there are altogether three in number. And what luck that there are no fewer. For that very morning, in the place of the serious bearded men, there now hung, in the same triangular formation, the portraits of Sándor Petőfi, Mihály Vörösmarty, and János Arany. It was as if no one else's portraits had ever hung on the wall of the police station. My father suddenly felt very calm. He delighted in these portraits. Among the three, he of course hung up Petőfi first, and of course in the middle, for he was the one who said to hang all the kings. And Petőfi couldn't be mad at this little joke, because after a short while, he saw János Arany, his old friend, right next to him; Arany saw Petőfi too, but he didn't believe his eyes. What are you staring at? asked Petőfi. Close your eyes, he said, if you don't believe, if you don't believe that it is I; and ask your heart, for surely that shall give reply . . . After his happy stupefaction, however, Arany was overcome by his usual habits of renunciation. For surely of an evening, sorrowful Petőfi he did see, indeed by day as well, as he slipped in through the window and caressed his brow, but in vain the tale is spun that his friend may yet appear; he knows what this means, and he knows too that the shadows ascending from the grave never brought life.

Vörösmarty, who hung from the third nail, became even more agitated. He wanted to know everything immediately, never running out of questions, yet it was not Petőfi or Arany whom he interrogated but my father. Tell me, he said to him, what is going on now in the Magyar homeland. At this my father shrugged his shoulders, and he answered, People are eating, drinking, and singing. Vörösmarty took this as sarcasm, but still he tried to get an answer out of my father. In the end it was never too difficult to get someone to start complaining in the Magyar homeland. So he asked, There are no problems? No specter of troubles for which we must atone? There are always specters of troubles. And sometimes there is atonement. Now, however, the men who jumped out of the old Ikarusz bus that just braked in front of the police station, equipped with crowbars, were getting ready to make my father atone. They were the specters of troubles. An ominous society. They pushed in the garden gate; yelling, they began to beat the door down; it nearly gave way. "They're going to kill your father!" That was not their voice, but my mother's. She ran to the back of the house. I was right at her heels, but the miners got there before us. They smashed the table and the radio to pieces, they smashed the electric bulb on the wall, and they yelled, "Now you'll pay! Now the impertinent ones shall pay, the good-for-nothings! If he disobeys the law, he'll get stuck on a branch, he will pay in this world and in the next!"

The policemen, three in number apart from my father, stood in a row before the smashed table as if they had been ordered to report to a superior. Tin soldiers, have you pissed your pants? Each of their right hands was stuck in their pockets, grasping the loaded pistol. Self-control. Self-control. My mother embraced me and squeezed me to herself, her body swallowed mine. The crowbars were still taking their revenge on the objects: on the chairs, the painted cabinets, whose glass shards shattered everywhere. The blood ran down the hand of one of the policemen in a thin streak. And Petőfi, just as he had done ever since May 1848, heard the trombone sounding the alarm, and he saw the sea of blood. Mourning and blood. For mourning and blood shall be the fate of the Hungarian people, and God has ordered poets so to lead! he cried out, and with that he jumped down from the wall. Despite being a scrawny chap, if his nose sensed the scent of blood, and the fate of the Hungarian nation held out the prospect of teaching a little lesson, nothing could restrain him—but the nail on which his portrait hung was too much for him, poor thing.

In the meantime, the police station had run out of objects that could be smashed. There remained only the heads of the policemen—from which, in actuality, one or two things should have been beaten out—but the miners' leader, a spunky little man with a broad head, believed much less than the three bearded men in the possibilities of education, and so he promised instead that he would smash their skulls to bits. He emphatically spit into my father's eye, and he began to tear off the stars from his regimental facing, the star-shaped buttons from his jacket. A ceremonial demotion. The drum roll sounded, the trumpets blared. The policemen stood there in their battered uniforms, their heads bent, in the middle of the battlefield, while the Hussars, in their blue procession, in their braided shakos rode their horses, their flags waving above.

"Who is that?" the leader of the miners snarled at my father suddenly, and he pointed at the middle picture, which, hearing the trumpet's blare, moved.

My father turned around, and his gaze met that of Petőfi.

"That one?" he asked.

"That one!" growled the miner, and with his crowbar he broke the glass of the picture.

The photograph behind the glass was also damaged, ripped along the right side of the face burning with a feverish glow.

"That is Sándor Petőfi."

It seemed that, drunk as he was, the leader of the men with the crowbars didn't know what to make of this name, because he demanded to know, with an emphasis in his voice which did not bode well, where this Sándor Petőfi lived.

Upon hearing this, the facial muscles on Vörösmarty's face began to convulse, then he broke out in loud laughter. It was a true nineteenth-century laughter, swelling and wild. In the end it was Petőfi who tore down the star from the heavens above our homeland while he voted with the majority in the national assembly concerning the military question, and that hot-headed actor had the impudence to encourage him to tear the "Summons" to pieces. Well now, let this jester gaze up to the heavens above our homeland! Where does his star hail from? However much it glimmers, it was washed off by a glass of bad brandy, and not even a blotch remained. For ever since the world has been the world, the heavens above our homeland have been cheered by the ardor of the patriots, and by brandy! Thus we too are the glittering August stars in the heavens above our homeland, we all plunge down. Vörösmarty laughed at that as he had never done before. He didn't even laugh—instead, hanging on the wall, he barked. On my father's face—he also penned verses now and then, birthday greetings and the like—not even a muscle twitched.

"He lives up on the hill," (my father pointed in the direction of the mountain), "next to the estate steward's house."

Next to the house of the steward, in a smaller house, was born the poet who was named as the chief of all Hungarian poets by not just anyone, but by Ferenc Kazinczy himself. And he was right, because the one who dipped his goose quill into the autobiographical ink bottle of Pál Rontó filled his readers' eternally empty guts not only with white loaves, milk bread, fried dough, and "Gypsy bread" but also with wonderful strudels, tasty doughnuts with dill and curd fillings too, and anyone who would dare to say after all this that he preferred to confer with the dead—those who had been and who were no more—truly would remain the chief of the poets. And as the men with the crowbars unconditionally wanted to beat in someone's head, that head could be none other than that of a Hungarian poet—that is to say, the head of poor József Gvadányi, even if the hussars, in the middle of beating him up, referred to him as bloody Petőfi.

And that is how the last Hungarian revolution began in Rudabánya. My father telephoned district headquarters in Edelény to ask for instructions, but he found no commander there. There was no knife yet in the heart of Lamberg, no noose around the neck of Latour, and still no one had the time to pick up the phone. It rang for a long time, it rang echoingly. And by the time the echo had died away, the air was filled with news. There were demonstrations and arrests in Miskolc, there were massacres in Pest, the Russians were advancing toward the river Tisza. It was impossible for everything to be over when it hadn't even begun! It hadn't begun, yes, but what hadn't begun? Well, everything. The revolution, dammit! Early that morning, between 100 and 150 miners from Rudabánya set off for Miskolc. Among them was the teacher Antal Bokor. The train crossed the Szuha valley with torturous lassitude; near Kálló it was held up for a good quarter of an hour. The men were impatient, and there were bursts of anger—they couldn't miss the revolution just because of a stuck rail switch! Finally they succeed in hauling out a rail worker. Antal Bokor doesn't understand what is carrying him away, he's cursing the filthy troupe of secret police agents the loudest—Now they're running the railway as well! In Miskolc the crowd marched from Rudás László Street up to the Zsolcai Gate to the front of police headquarters, its facade shorn of its red star by peace-loving hands the day before. The news had spread that after a few dozen university students had been released, the delegates of the student parliament negotiating inside had been arrested. The miners, coming from the direction of the Gömöri train station, arrived at the Zsolcai Gate at around 9:15 p.m., exactly the moment when the crowd suddenly surged against the building—people were pushing from behind—and shooting was heard in the front. According to some, the guards on duty shot at the ceiling of the entranceway to hold back the crowd; if this was true, it is doubtful they acted merely from fright but had received orders. In others' estimations, the explosions were not bullets but hand grenades: they flew from the hand of the wife of Imre Gáti, captain of state security, like a beautiful bunch of grapes, in one fine cluster. It is, however, a fact that at the end of October the detectives entrusted with the task of clarifying the course of events interrogated Mrs. Gáti, then released her, taking her back to her relatives in Hidasnémeti. Following the shelling, the policemen stationed on the second and third floors, as well as the State Protection authorities stationed by the entranceway, proceeded as if they'd been given the command to shoot, although István Balogh Vörös, the police captain, only gave the order to fire more warning shots. Despite this, the demonstrators found themselves under heavy machine-gun fire, and hand grenades exploded in the crowd.

The shooting caused panic not only outside but within the police headquarters itself. Gyula Gáti, police lieutenant colonel, stepped out of the toilet with a confused expression on his face because it had just occurred to him that ten years earlier, in the summer of 1946, a mob had lynched some black marketeers because they thought they were Jewish; he recalled the maimed bodies dragged behind the horse-drawn carts. He saw himself tied by the neck to a horse-drawn cart, and from that point on he was no longer a lieutenant colonel but simply a terrified Jew. After the round of fire, the crowd dispersed, but still remained near the police headquarters. Many in the crowd went to the soldiers in the barracks across the street for weapons and protection. The soldiers were getting ready to turn their weapons against the State Protection authorities; their officers could barely restrain them from besieging police headquarters. The police and the head of State Security decided to ask for help from the organizers of the revolution, the student parliament, and the workers' councils of the large factories, handing over their commandership to the Workers' Councils Committee. As, following the shooting, the human fence around the building had temporarily slackened, the delegates managed to reach the factories, but returned with only one member of the Home Guard, who was negotiating for the workers. It was decided that Lieutenant Gyula Gáti, still stricken with horror, should proceed, accompanied by the Home Guardsman, to the metallurgy works and try to negotiate with the leaders there. They did not get very far. Gáti changed into civilian clothes, but was recognized by several people in the crowd. Defensive warning shots were fired from the building, so he and the Home Guardsman were able to slip away momentarily. They escaped into the cellar of a nearby building but were immediately found; the crowd beat Gáti unconscious, then tied him by the neck to the back of a truck, just like the image of the events that had come to him a little while earlier, and he was dragged to the Palace of Music, where he was strung up.

All this can be precisely stated. But can the battered body of Gyula Gáti be seen now, some sixty-five years later, can the people felled in the crowd by machine-gun fire be seen as they fall down like ninepins? And if the eye cannot, then can imagination perceive this simultaneity? If it can perceive it, then we too must try to imagine: not only because otherwise we will not be able to understand why the pistol that the teacher Antal Bokor had taken to be repaired years ago in Ormosbánya, and had regularly cleaned with an oily rag ever since, was fired within a matter of minutes, but also because of this: if we cannot evoke before our own eyes at any time the possibility of a crowd being mowed down by machine-gun fire, that is, at the push of a button, just as in school we must know that two times two equals four, well, then what do we know in general, what do we even know about where we live, for surely in most cities on our planet from time to time there are lynchings, from time to time the trees are adorned with corpses, and that unbearably dense, gelatinous mass, kneaded together from the material of pitiful human life, is reduced by means of machine-gun fire.

So let us now imagine how the body of Gyula Gáti was dragged from the Zsolcai Gate to the Palace of Music, a distance of approximately two kilometers. He is dragged, tied to a truck bumper, his uniform already torn off, a filthy blood-scone, a blood-purée the color of dried plums, a blackened blood-purée, the Jew pig, State Protection manure. At the very most, we can only imagine all this. But teacher Antal

Bokor watched this beautiful, ceremonial dragging—this rite of revenge and anger—with his own eyes. He stood by the Zsolcai Gate, not far from the entrance to Ady Endre Street, in front of a balconied apartment house. Just then the truck passed before him. He looked at the body, which was no longer a body, and as the truck rumbled on, his gaze became fixated on the knot hitched to the bumper—the other end was tied around Gáti's neck. It was a simple, regular knot, nothing complicated about it, pulled tight by the hand of a strong man. The attention of Antal Bokor was often absorbed by such minor details. There were about a dozen or so people running after the truck: men, older people too. Later on his memory of the event strangely muted this sequence; he heard neither the rumbling of the truck engine nor the yelling of the people running behind, as if everything he saw were occurring beneath a transparent membrane. That membrane, cutting off his hearing and excluding him, if not definitively then for years to come, from the scene, was drawn around him by the reports of his own pistol. He fired three times into the horse's eye. One, two, three. By the time the third shot rang out, causing the center of the horse's skull to crack open, the membrane sealed shut, enclosing him inside, rendering the events that had occurred repeatable at any time.

There were many who were cursing Gáti, or what was left of him by the Zsolcai Gate. Traitor. Rotten murderer. Not even a Hungarian. They dragged him over to the monument of Soviet soldiers, where the noose was placed upon his neck. At the base of the monument, there already lay a cadaver: a brown, short-legged, sturdy horse. A cold-blooded Belgian. A stalwart Brabant draft horse. Soda water, get your soda water here! The horse was sprayed with gunfire. Its blood was flowing; weeping, the cart driver cut its neck. Get your soda water here! Now Gáti was being rolled around in the muddy cold blood of the draft horse.

"Animals! These aren't people! These are animals!"

Who was that? Who said that? He wasn't thinking about the horse, that much was sure.

Yet another Jew. Won't we ever run out of them?

Lajos Freimann, who in the subsequent documents would appear as a "civilian victim," elsewhere as a "button hawker," arrived in Miskolc having set off from Debrecen in a gray GAZ-M20 Pobeda with three companions on the evening of October 25. What were they doing there? Were they doing a little business on the side at a time like that? Were they also working as State Protection agents? Freimann went to the toilet in the hotel where they were staying, and on the wall he saw this inscription: "Death to the Jews!" He asked the head-waiter to remove it. But he didn't know what kind of expression he should have on his face when he said this. Especially now, when . . . For God's sake, don't get nervous! The next day, in front of the monument to the Soviet soldiers, Gyula Gáti's murderers seized Freimann as well. They too saw something—they could tell he was a Jew. Gáti's older brother. A State Protection major, God dammit! Freimann with his three companions had begun to run back to the hotel, and he was caught there when two waiters blocked the entrance; the men in pursuit caught up with them. Freimann was dragged back to the monument. A beautiful high obelisk. After several attempts, they hanged him from the pedestal of the monument, the rope breaking twice underneath the weight of the heavy, convulsing body. The eternal blundering that comes along with murder. Now all that remained was to pull down Freimann's trousers. If he was circumcised, that meant they'd killed a Jew. He was circumcised. The skin of the glans, stiffened from suffocation, was taut and gleaming. Not too big of a tool. A Jewish prick. You wanted to see it, no? A death-stiffened Jewish prick glimmers beneath the obelisk.

And then. What could happen then? What could happen? A shot rings out.

Teacher Antal Bokor shoots into the horse's glassy eye. The glass shatters. The dead horse is blinded. Its skull breaks open. And the shots ringing out, sealing Antal Bokor within that membrane, also create order in the empty time outside of the membrane: the copper plate on the wall clock swings back and forth, once again the dark brown wood of the clock has a voice that can be heard. My father walks along Lajos Kossuth Street toward the school, and he already knows that he will not arrest his friend. He will report that the pistol repaired by the mechanic in Ormosbánya was a toy pistol with a cartridge. But this time, he won't be able to get out of the story so easily. On the twenty-sixth of October, in the late evening, as the train is taking the miners back to Miskolc, Antal Bokor pays a visit to my father. He tells him what happened at the Zsolcai Gate, reassuring my father that no harm can come to him and advising him to join the miners' workers' council as a community commanding officer. My mother brings in dinner, the bean soup left over from lunch is steaming—she hates, she hates this place where she lives. And what she hears now about the lynching in Miskolc, she will hear for decades to come. "There has to be order," my father says, "that is the most important thing." He doesn't talk about the men with the crowbars, but he's thinking about them. A few days later the Russians march into the village. Four Russians riding in an open UAZ military vehicle. It comes to a stop in front of the police station. For the time being there are no new pictures on the wall; that will have to wait until everything is cleared up—the old ones, the poets, were taken down a long time ago.

Now once again the three blotches are creating an eyesore on the wall, and the Russians make my father stand directly beneath them. Among the Russians, there's also a Hungarian, he speaks Hungarian. He asks my father why he switched his allegiance to the workers' council when he was a police officer. He calls him to account. He's curious. He could shoot him if he wanted to, but for now he's only accusing him.

My father gives him the same answer that he gave to the teacher Antal Bokor. Order must be kept. And here, in the village, there was no lynching. Not a hair on anyone's head was touched.

And this was the only answer which satisfied the Russians. In the end, man has not changed much since the birth of the first human couple, who heard the words of the Lord when they went into the garden, and with one single word fulfilled their political mission to rule over the earth with a word of language, and this word was none other than *order*. "Seder" is how the young children of creation pronounced it. The man interpreting said, "Paryadok. On sledil za paryadokom." And that was enough—the UAZ drove off, just as it had arrived. The district comrades returned, the ones who had fled across the border to Slovakia on October 24. They saved their own chickenshit lives. Now, though, they came back, and they asked the same thing as the Russians. Only because they were Hungarians, and because they were the comrades from Edelény, the question sounded different. And my father answered completely differently. He didn't speak about order—that was precisely what he didn't speak about. "Kak tu skazesh pa vengerskij 'paryadok'? Nikak, nikak." My father was overcome with rage, and he had a question of his own. He asked: "I was here, but where were all of you? Where the hell were all of you?" And with this question he submitted his application to hand in his weapon. To confiscate his uniform wasn't so easy though. So he wouldn't be tried before a military tribunal, so he wouldn't be put away for years, he had to do something. In the end, it wasn't even such a big thing. He had to arrest Antal Bokor, who had taken part, in Miskolc, in the bestial murder of Gyula Gáti. They reminded my father of the affair with the pistol that had taken place a few years ago—they knew all about it in Edelény. That he had mistaken a Parabellum for a toy pistol. What a blunder! There could be problems if this came up during Antal Bokor's hearing. And it probably was going to be mentioned, because they were going to have to explain to the comrades in Miskolc where the teacher had gotten the pistol that he had fired in front of police headquarters. There were witnesses to the fact that he had shot the guard first: the guard staggered, then shot into the ceiling. There are always witnesses for everything. That is order. They could even find something against my father if they wanted to. But why would they want to? They could completely forget about that pistol-repair business. As long as . . .

As long as.

There was no need to finish the sentence. My father sets off once again beneath the trees arching over Kossuth Lajos Street, he's in no hurry, for the school day isn't over yet, and in one half hour, when the wall clocks in the village all strike two, he will accompany the teacher Antal Bokor, who will be granted amnesty only in 1963, to the police station. And the teacher, before he steps out of the school building, will ask my father if he knows what the eye of a dead horse looks like. The eye of a dead Brabant draft horse. Soda water—come get your soda water! What it looks like when a bullet is whizzing at it straight out of the Parabellum.

7
Secret Theater

If I stood on my tiptoes, and really stretched myself out, I could see, above the plank fencing of the pigsty, the clouds of the autumn sky. They were wind-swept clean shawls, as if waving farewell. As I attempted, through vigorous thrusts, to clutch at the top of the planks and pull my body across the fencing—wishing to liberate myself from my captivity— the air was forced out from my lungs through the effort, and every attempt ended with me shamefully plopping back onto the ground. That morning at dawn the overly fattened pigs had been driven from the sty so that the knife could be plunged into their necks outside. The thick mud, mixed with manure, was splashed across my buckled shoes, my cotton hose. I don't know why it was exactly that my shoes and my stockings made me such a miserable sight, and it wasn't that earlier moment, when, with my mother's consent, my father grabbed me by the arm and dragged me over to the sty, or even earlier, when my mother tied my ankle to the table leg, because she'd had enough of my running around all over the place and getting myself covered in dirt; it was true, though, that in the following moment, seized by a fit of rage, I shook the pigsty's plank door, closed from outside, and I screamed dreadful things. I don't remember what. Then, exhausted,

I was quiet; I crouched by the base of the planks. I no longer bothered with the mud. Maybe I was even happy that
my shoes, my stockings had become completely filthy. They
became muddy, not me. I have nothing to do with it. I have
nothing to do with anything that happens to me. They're the
ones doing it: they're the guilty ones. Even if they don't know
what they're doing. And I'm not even going to plead for a
temporary reprieve. I have no tongue for it, it was cut out,
paralyzed. The cat stole it. Or it wasn't paralyzed, they didn't
cut it out, I can still talk but not to them, not for them—but
then to whom? Who is going to hear what I have to say: I'm
filthy, and I no longer have the right to be clean. Because this
morning this was the place where the pigs were, from which
they were dragged out, legs tied up, and now it's my place,
they've shut me up here. From now on this is my place. I
must engrave it into my memory. It was needed in my memory. And from that moment on, so I say, although there is
no beginning and no end to all this, I became incapable of
conveying myself to others. I understood something that
was unfamiliar to me. The whole day long my parents never
heard my words—I believe they were satisfied with me, the
shining fruit of their upbringing, and as my grades at school
had also visibly improved, they were even proud. They were
ashamed of me at most if, at the market, or when visiting, an
adult, acquaintance, or relative asked me something, initiat-
ing the kind of conversation adults try to have with children.
Instead of replying, at such times my eyes dissected the
questioning face, tearing away the stitches located between
the nose, mouth, and eyes—of which they themselves were
unaware—so preoccupied were they with their own unfathomable benevolence, their wish to do good, and their pity

for such a smart little girl, who, it appeared, was far more timid than she needed to be.

There was no reason to pity me though, because it was at that time that speech began to loosen up in me, except that I didn't speak to the others, and I wasn't speaking to you yet, dear reader, but only to myself, and ceaselessly, in a double language. The first tongue was that of stories that I told myself. They were gloomy tales, but they all, without exception, ended well. The second tongue was that of my emotions, it was labyrinthine, dark, and full of obstacles: I could not take even one step in this tongue without gaining new wounds. By now, though, I've lost that tongue: it perished, or dissolved in other languages I learned later on. This was not true for that tongue of stories without end. They branched out mostly from books, taking up residence in a picture which hung above my bed. If I think back on it, I see myself lying on the bed: I'm reading, completely submerged in a book, as if I had moved to a foreign city; outside it's dark, the rain is falling, the kind of rain which makes the days seem at once both infinite and monotonous. And this infinity— in the minutes before falling asleep, when I put down the book—suddenly narrowed, filling me with unspeakable delight. In my nook on the second floor of our house, across from my bed, was a picture on the wall which, at such times, opened before me, calling me to step among its peculiar figures. Of course the picture was a copy, a cheap reproduction affixed to cardboard. My father had gotten it from a rag-and-bone man from Putnok, or at least that's what he said when he came home with it tucked beneath his arm, because he had a tendency to vanish at that time, when we moved into a smaller house in Rudabánya, and he, finally relinquishing uniforms, took a job as a janitor at the mine. The janitor had no other task than to sweep away the eternal dust from the front of the mining engineers' building and attend to the crossing gate for trucks driving in and out. My father was not satisfied with his position, particularly after my mother got a job at the state orphanage: she cooked for them, bringing home food in stacked aluminum food containers. My father said there was no need for that. He came home from his absences and his occasional disappearances stinking of brandy, but from his coat or bag he always conjured up some kind of gift: lettuce, gloves, or stockings. Thus for a while he was able to pacify my mother. It wasn't so easy, though, for him to purchase lasting grace for himself. My grandmother was right—he was a lazy man. And if he were only lazy! He drinks as well. He has the nerve to show up at home after two days of drinking, who the hell knows what he was up to. Why can't he just go back to where he came from? The curses and the accusations poured out of my mother; she couldn't stop herself. She cursed my father because of what he had become. A nothing, a big piece of nothing. She cursed his drinking companions, she cursed his brothers, too, she cursed the fact that he'd come back home from Hamburg, what a shame. She cursed, but not too loudly, only muttering, until a bitter pained shouting broke out of my father for my mother to stop already, he knew very well that he was a scoundrel, he knew he was a nothing, but may God smite the heavens upon him, stop already. He was yelling, beside himself. Couldn't she leave him alone already! All the same, one day he would shoot himself. Although my father no longer had a pistol. Still, I was convinced he was going to shoot himself in the head. In one of my schoolbooks, I'd seen a picture in which Lajos Batthyány was kneeling, his hands spread open, in front of the rifles; he was about be shot in the head. You could see how his skull was about to be filled with holes, he had a very beautiful domed head, and in a moment crimson blood would come gushing out of it. I didn't understand how my mother could want this. Why did she say that she didn't care if my father wanted to shoot himself in the head? Someone lies on the ground, they drag him away, the splotches of blood are strewn with sand. Why did she say that he wouldn't be able to blackmail her with that?

When my father calmed down, he took out the present he'd brought home for me. By now he dared bring presents only to me: the more he had on his conscience, the more beautiful they were. And so a picture depicting the tiny square of an old town ended up on the wall opposite my bed. The many balconies and windows of the two- and three-story townhouses looked down on the square; I counted them anew every evening, and the final sum varied, depending on how many windows and balconies I lost track of or located in the picture. I was certain this small town truly existed; my imagination determined that I would have to seek it out in Germany or the Netherlands. The square was in no way the tabernacle of the sun that the painter would have depicted in a similar square of a city in a more southern clime; its brightness, washed through with vigorous pastel colors, did not have an unequivocal source. This and the silent, sorrowful manner of the depiction meant that the square resembled, more than anything else, the cardboard construction of a theater backdrop: the men and the women who were painted there, however—who got dressed and undressed, ac-

cording to their respective roles, in their rooms backstage—
struck me as being somewhat more real, just enough so as
not to be performing their roles like puppets. The painter
had condemned them to repeat their rehearsed scenes in
my presence every evening before falling asleep, so that not
a single day would be forfeited from time, so they would be
waiting forever in this immutability.

In the darkest corner of the picture a short-legged, thin
man, covered in black, was leaning over, a kind of sterile,
deformed creature fleeing from every gaze, although right at
this moment he hurried to his own demise toward a youngster who had just appeared in a side street. In the next moment—which the painter did not paint—the man in black,
his hair growing wildly around his red ears sticking out beneath his top hat, was exposed to the youngster's detested
gibes; perhaps even the victim of his prank. As, however,
this scene repeated itself daily, it no longer disturbed anyone, no one even noticed it, least of all that braggart, who,
in a bright entranceway, was courting a young beautiful girl
in his usual manner, gossiping incessantly about his adventures, and mainly about all the duels he had fought, without, of course, ever wishing to wound his opponent, for he'd
only done so for the sake of honor. The girl was excessively
amused by this prattle, but she remained undeceived. The
painter rendered her face just a shade paler than that of the
braggart, leaving no doubt that this gentle and open face
would forever remain an unattainable secret to the man, as
her laughter was borne away.

The other performers in the picture were not too trou-
bled by such scenes. Showing off their wondrous theatrical
garments, they lived such rich lives in those windows and

balconies that a cheap spectacle like this couldn't hold their attention. Some spoke in pairs, others in groups of three or four beneath the painted heavens, young ladies and gentlemen, and mature women as well. News was shared from one window to the other, absorbed in the intricate life of the town, in the never-ending scrutiny of business, familial, and especially amorous relations. They gossiped, casually stripping some of love-worthy traits, and just as casually exalting others—they shot arrows into each other's hearts, they flirted, courted each other, flew into rages, or broke out in sobs, which nobody considered childish. And after this or that well-played scene they happily applauded each other, nor was any window or balcony miserly with recognition; nor was I miserly with recognition, I who every night before sleeping viewed their curious performances. This was a theater, a true theater, my theater of every evening. If one evening I might have commanded those ladies and gentlemen to interrupt their performance and retire to their darkened rooms, they would have been consumed by infinite sadness. The residents of this little town came back to life only while this performance was being staged—otherwise they were dead—and as they stepped onto the stage they forgot that everything that ever could have happened to them had already happened many times over, making their performance nothing more than an amusing and hopeless masquerade. The painter knew this, for surely he was the one who created this square for them, whose authentic counterpart he clearly saw as being in Germany or the Netherlands—he enclosed them in a window frame or on a balcony, never allowing them to fall out of time; he was the one who made them so weightless and unhappy. And because he was

141

sorry for them, he sent someone to that square whom they were truly not expecting. The picture depicts that moment, as, in the middle of the square, there stands a postman. His bag nearly bursting with letters, he looks up to the windows, but what was written on his face by that painter—what can be read from that face—cannot be seen by me, the viewer of this picture, nor by you, dear reader, because the painter shows the postman's face only to those standing in the windows and on the balconies. And there are only a few among them, at this moment, who take notice of him, as in the windows and on the balconies the chitchat continues, the wooing, the endless tattle of names. And as for those who do notice him—a young woman, whom almost everyone considers a neatly turned, pleasant-tempered creature but without particularly strong appeal, and a gentleman, already not entirely young, who most likely nurses sentiments toward that young woman he has yet to unveil to himself—well, both of them stare fixedly at the postman with such stupefied expressions on their faces, from which once again it is not possible to tell if they have taken in some fatal misfortune or, on the contrary, have been greeted by the news of a long-awaited escape. The final blow of death, disappearance—or a life not yet lived? Truly, the appearance of the postman—which reaches the performers every evening, always unprepared—is an integral part of this play. And in a moment excitement will once again prevail on the square, pairs and groupings of three will come apart, everyone will begin speaking at once. They want to know what's happened. To whom has the postman come? Who sent him? What news does he bring? Some fall into hysterics, others are suddenly tranquil, screams are heard from all directions, and with this wondrous chaos, the play comes to an end.

This was my own secret theater, the theater of every evening. It was mine—the actors of the Dutch or German town played for me, the painter had painted them for me, for me, who, like them, was surrounded, enclosed by the constraints of a life fabricated against me—although at the time I still hardly sensed that, I still wasn't aware, and yet still I slipped into my room, between its walls every evening, as into a warm quilted jacket in the winter cold, and I fell asleep seeing beneath my closed eyes the picture that I'd received from my father.

But my eyes preserved another image as well, that of the pigsty's mud. This too was a picture I received from my father, although even today I do not blame him, I do not reproach him for the fact that I became covered with dirt. If my mother was angry or weeping, or if she was quarreling, if she found the cause of her unhappy life in me, then my father stood next to her, his rage suddenly grown tenfold, his face blue and purple, and now I say that it was not him, this was not my father, but a frightfully strong, wretched being who suffered because his strength and his wretchedness were knotted together with my mother's wounded nerves. Yes, even today I'm still angry at my mother, and I'm ashamed as well, because even though I deserved the punishment, indeed I deserved a lot, she should have known that she shouldn't have punished me, not in that way, because whenever I had to go into the sty with a bowl of pig swill or a basket of maize, I was overcome with dread. I couldn't stand the smell of the pigsty or of pork; in vain did my father tell me to eat it or I would remain weak. "You will be weak, my daughter," he said, "and you will always be sick." I turned the meat around in my mouth, and swallowed it without chewing.

The lives of both my father and my mother were unknown labyrinths to me, and so it has remained, no matter what I say about it. In the depths of their wretchedness an unmanageable anger seethed, mixed with arrogance and resignation, obligatory affection, and perhaps even some love. But love is what I know the least about, if there was any love between them at all; and what I know is merely something I've made up for myself, whom else would I have made it up for: it was necessary for me, only me, so that I wouldn't become completely lost in this labyrinth, so that I might present myself with a gift, one they forgot to give me, one they were incapable of giving, so deeply were they permeated with this wretchedness lacking words. The city too was drenched in this wretchedness, as if in a kind of bile-flavored, poisonous brine: it flowed down from the walls, gave its taste to the bodies, the eyes swam in this brine and the children were born out of it, every throat was filled with it, and it made anyone who tried to speak mute. And yet I still wanted to speak, if not here then in another city, another city I made up for myself; but for that I needed a kind of grace which could emerge only from here. And I don't know why, but I hoped for this grace from my father—yes, even from him: his love would have been that gift which, it now appears with the passage of time, I had to invent for myself, and I did invent it, just as I invented that city into which someone bearing unexpected tidings turned up unexpectedly in one of its hidden small squares surrounded by three- and four-story burghers' houses.

I remember that when I learned how to ride a bicycle (of course my father's bicycle, which was too big for me), at the end of the street, where I had to turn off toward the large abandoned lot known as Bagolyvár, I didn't know what to do: should I brake, or should I try to turn? The handlebars began to twist beneath my hands, and I lost my balance. The sidewalk was too close, I plunged on to its edge and broke my arm. I was convinced it was broken. The pain seared through me. I scrambled to my feet and saw the flesh cut open on my arm, the blood gushing out. I had nothing to bandage it. My arm was shaking, I couldn't even hold it because I had to somehow push my father's bicycle home. I saw that there was no particular damage to the bicycle. The reflector light in front had broken off, and the handlebar was bent. I wasn't worried about that; instead I was afraid what would happen if my parents found out what I'd done to myself, what my mother would say. It was as if my body weren't even mine but hers. My arms, my legs, my neck, my head, every part of my body was hers. And now I had disassembled it, I had ruined, broken a part of it. But the pain was mine. I was happy for the pain; I was also happy that when I stepped into the garden gate it was not her but my father who stood before me. He stood there, saw that I was covered in blood, and without asking anything at all slapped me hard across the face. Then I burst out crying. I didn't understand anything, but I cried and cried, and I had good reason to.

And it was good. The tears ran down my neck. And it was good that my arm hurt. I always bore pain very well: dentists always praised me for that, even my mother was proud of it. And it was good that my father had taken care of everything with one slap across the face. Because now my mother couldn't say anything—my father, with that slap, had anticipated her, now she had to remain mute, she had to accompany me to the doctor, mute, because now the fact that I broken my arm was forgiven. At the doctor's a nice thick cast was placed on my arm, reaching up to my elbow, and everyone immediately realized what had happened. I could not wash by myself. My mother stood me in an enamel washbasin and soaped me down from head to toe, I only had to stand still and make sure the cast didn't get wet. Her hand quickly slid across my back, my stomach, every evening with the same motions, one by one she confiscated my shoulders, my hips, my neck, and she washed my loins as well. She worked roughly, as if cleaning an object in haste. Still, I offered no resistance; somehow it was good even like this. I had obtained forgiveness, and not even the roughness of her touch could change that.

Decades later, those evening washings came to my mind once again. My mother was now old, with ulcers on her legs. "Leave it alone," she said, "I'll do it myself." She wouldn't let me wipe down the area around the purple, damp wounds with a moist sponge, she wouldn't let me rub ointment on it. It caused her pain simply for me to see her like this, for me to be aiding her, bringing her socks in bed, helping her up. In her old age, by the time that wretchedness without words had wreaked the same ruination upon her that it did upon everyone, once again she became the adolescent girl who walked behind the house to look for chamomile and potassium permanganate to disinfect herself, because for weeks on end she had not moved her bowels, and there was bleeding in her intestines. She was ashamed that her body was ill. She no longer had any memories, only her distended, sickly body, those two ulcerated legs, her useless joints, and outside in the cemetery was a grave, the grave of my father, which she could not get to.

To go out to a grave. To weed the flowerbed, to adjust what needs to be adjusted, to stand around a bit in front of the name on the gravestone. To stand there, instead of . . . She missed this. Her face became bloated just like the faces I'd seen all around me in childhood, bloated faces, faces without memory, made of some material that was not human; not only were the faces of the old people like that, but young peoples' faces too, the faces of young women and men, as if their task had been to work themselves out of the world imperceptibly and methodically, to work out from the world the very last remnants of grace. My mother and father were kneaded from the material of this work, a material that was not human; and yet there were still moments between them that were easeful: of unexpected snowfall, moments of rest when you would just gaze out through the window, and everything was good. But that haughtiness of my mother's, wounded many times over, which over the years only drew an even thicker shell around her, prevented her from expunging her own accusations against my father. Therefore, without even being aware of it, and as it were deciding the status of their relationship for me, she compelled me a priori to a secret sense of shared fate with my father, to come to expect understanding and compassion from him.

And on that morning too, when I was beginning to sink down into that inexhaustible inner speech, my father arranged for me not to be at home, so I would not have to watch as he slaughtered the animal dragged out from the sty and thrown onto the ground. He told me to run to the police station and ask them if they wanted any liver, kidney, or giblets for lunch; if so, they could send someone over to us with a pot. The road to the police station went by Bagolyvár. Today there is a school there, a long, one-story yellow building with a sports field. There the boys are kicking the ball, a skinny short little boy standing between the goalposts, and now two soccer balls are coming at him at once: one is a modern soccer ball, covered in polyurethane; the other is an old one, yellow and brown, made of strips of hide, each three fingers' width. The balls fly toward him, one of them touches the goalpost, the other slips between his legs; he can't defend the goalpost. The old soccer ball was supposedly made of pig hide. If another boy hadn't gone after it, it would have bounced into the road. The new soccer ball bangs against the fence, making it clatter. Behind, the girls are playing hopscotch on the cinder track. They jump back and forth from square to square—the rules never change, only the clothes; we jumped from square to square when there was no school at all at Bagolyvár, no buildings, only a deserted lot, in the summer a sea of dust, in the fall the mud bath.

On that morning, it being Sunday, only local children were playing at Bagolyvár; they were pallid, skin and bones, stupid. At other times I wouldn't have stayed with them to run back and forth around the quadrangle of dust. The material of the village, the dry air that smelled like iron, the blistered, broken cement, the garbage, and the cigarette smoke were all washed together into a heavy mass by the infrequent rains, a mass with neither memories nor future; these children of the Bagolyvár were made of that too. And yet now I stayed with them, even though I was filled with anxiety, because I knew I was doing something I wasn't supposed to do. I was not obeying. My throat dried out; now it really was as if every last drop of water had been wrung out of me. I too was made of dust: my hair was nothing but dust, and my dress too. I don't recall how the time passed. By the time I got to the police station, it was late afternoon. I asked them if they wanted any liver. They laughed and said my father had sent it much earlier, they'd eaten lunch long ago and had even washed up.

I knew what was coming next. The stitches had broken loose between my mother's nose, her eyes, and her mouth, her face had come apart, and I was incapable of holding it together. Her mouth was yelling, "Oh, look, so the young lady has come home! Because that's how much you can rely on her," and her eyes said, "I will destroy you," and her nose, her nose said nothing, it merely snuffed its rage from the heavens. And my father seemed ten times as enraged as my mother. Was it really so important for the policemen to get their share of the feast? It's been a long time since my father worked with them. Now he sweeps the courtyard in front of the miners' engineering building. Or is this about something else entirely? And this something else, do they understand what it is? My father's face grows nice and red, it's beautiful when it's red from anger, almost as red as beetroot, and he's grabbing my arm, he's pulling me along the long, slightly rising courtyard. How does he know that this is what he must do now? What dictates this to him? From the loamy ground of the courtyard everything living has been trampled down, there is neither blade of grass nor dried stalk, a child's bathtub has been put out in front of the house, and in it is the pig meat, cut up and still warm; the sides of the tub are bloody. What inscribed this into my father's nerves, and when? He drags me over to the pigsty, this is not me, not me, not me. So now this too is a Babel? He squeezes my arm, his fingers press into my arm, it hurts. The decaying wall of the house also hurts. Its cracks, its roughness hurt me, scraping against my skin. And my mother's voice also hurts, because my mother's mouth is always speaking. Her words hurt; I am nothing but abrasions. But now it is my father who is doing it. From him shall come the disproportionate punishment. In a basin are the bones, in another basin the remains of the innards, the lungs, and some pieces of liver. Blood runs over the edge of the basin, blood and bile. Now my father is doing this, my father's hand is dry and strong. He grabs my arm. And the bolt on the wooden plank door to the pigsty clicks shut behind me. I am imprisoned here, now I shall be imprisoned forever. I stand on my tiptoes. If I really stretch myself out, I can see the clouds in the autumn sky. Slowly it is growing dark; I wait for my father to come for me and let me out.

8

The Mouths of the Sacks Are Loosened

We are the fools of Babel. We could also be the comic dancers of existence, but only unwittingly, leaving mirth to grow by itself, like a flower planted by no one. You, dear reader, who have accompanied me until now, you know this, and you also know that I do not speak of unrestrained jesters, who, like Arabian thoroughbreds, groan and blow the air out of their nostrils, forcing all kinds of bestial whimpering so as to extort more good humor out of the spirits residing within—instead I speak of those who make the sorrows within them laugh, and as the sorrows belong as much to the world as to them, everything and everyone who ever sees or hears them laughs with them. This is the greatest gift which can be bestowed upon a mortal being by nature. And Carlita, the daughter of Signor del Filato, had been granted an abundant share of this gift. It was enough for me to hear in the morning from some corner of the house her warm, dear voice: my mood was gladdened immediately. If I awoke that day with dark thoughts, she chased them away; my sluggish organs, arising only with difficulty, happily completed their tasks, although I never would have admitted even to myself, for any sum of money, that it was Carlita's nearness, like a melodious echo, that filled me with this pleasant mood—instead I attributed it to the favorable climate of The Hague, well, and of course to the approach of spring: I decided that I would not shorten my stay here in the house of Signor del Filato.

And I had no reason for haste. I insulated myself from news of the war inasmuch as I could, hoping the French and the Germans might spare The Hague, that it might escape Brussels's unfortunate fate, and thus I would be able to live out my time in the house of Signor del Filato tranquilly, whatever might await me there. Particularly since the war was in its final year. Supplies were running low, the troops were marching back and forth in Flanders, only engaging in hostilities if confrontation could not be avoided, and although idiotic lust for glory had not yet expired in a few charming second lieutenants, and the eternally unruly ones, the soldiers no longer desired to inflict damage upon each other, only as much as was fitting, to make it seem as if a war were still taking place. Thus it seemed the French and the Germans had come to an agreement: the ultimate goal of war was neither murder nor enemy defeat—for that, the papers and quills of the peacemakers were already lined up— but pillage, *schnäppchen,* as the Germans put it, a good bargain, or, as the French termed it, *déprédation,* and therefore no city could feel secure, or trust in its own luck. This was equally true of The Hague, but the burghers of The Hague were wise. They stood with neither the French nor the Germans, remunerating each side amply for the protection of their city; they even traded with them under unfavorable conditions, so that if they were not exactly getting off cheap, apart from a few harmless break-ins the city was able to maintain its particular advantage until the end of the war. In this last year, however, even the granaries of The Hague were beginning to empty. The citizens were obliged to bake their bread from sorghum or grains swept up from the cellar floor because for years the soldiers had been plundering the crops down to the last stalk, and the price at which the residents of the city could repurchase some small amount was, in that final, chaotic phase of the war, as high as the heavens. The news of the armistice was received as a kind of redemption, as it was termed, in the spring of 1748.

Still, though, it was winter, the month of February, the sun rose late, but by midday the sky had frequently cleared, the light of spring penetrated the clothes hung out to dry, white linens hanging from the cords strung up between the houses. I too could dress in clean garments: Carlita mended my ripped shirts and stockings, and other signs of her care reached me as well, if in no other manner than her sending the last of the fragrant rennet apples, put aside last autumn, to my upstairs room. Is it a wonder then, that in the house of Signor del Filato I had found a kind of tranquillity of which earlier I had not the least suspicion? Although if the light had already begun to glimmer at noon, due to the proximity of the house across the street, it didn't even so much as lay a fringe around the gloom of my upstairs quarters. So for the time being I gladly sat in front of the window: it was almost like a turret window, not least because those minutes of noon sunlight were followed without warning by rainy, mood-destroying clouds, which, particularly in these cities, narrowed the sky above so closely so as to entice no one outside for a stroll. In the house of Signor del Filato, from one day to the next I began to conduct myself like someone who his whole life had lived in a small city of his own, never moved from there, and had no care for what took place outside of the city walls. I soon realized that such a person is much more susceptible to prevailing atmospheric conditions than the worker in the fields, or indeed the soldier marching with his troops from one place to another. Thanks to these walls, weather is merely a question of mood for him, unlike those for whom rain means untraversed roads, mud-stuck carts, or over-burdened plows. And so I became an idle and tranquil burgher of the city, and I cannot claim this change was not to my liking. I believed I still had plenty of time to get to know The Hague and its environs.

Standing in front of the window, I observed the life—not exactly clamorous—of the street and surrounding houses; my gaze was happy to glide farther along the steep red roofs. All my previous travels—the dark operating table of poor Master Fröschlin, the incursions of Frangipan's regiment, and the wartime escapes—began at once to sink down to the depths of this unchanging prospect, as if everything had taken place behind a heavy curtain which would never again be raised; and yet at the same time I sensed ever more clearly that these events had been but a mere preparation for something else, and the curtain was once again about to rise.

And when this happened, when that curtain finally moved—and a glimmer of light, albeit not too much, was thrown on those environs which today I might heedlessly designate as *my world* (although since it could not have been that, I will content myself by saying that some light was shed on a world concealed from my eyes until then)—I still behaved like someone being led about by a rope. One morning, from the end of the street, where the facades of the burghers' houses, somewhat larger and wealthier than Signor del Filato's residence, looked out on to an open square, a racket of lively drumrolls, ratchets, whistles, and cymbals broke into my upstairs room. The noise was hellishly amplified in the narrow street; awakening from a dream, I believed that in the dawn hours, while its burghers slept, The Hague's luck had finally run out, and the French or Germans had invaded the city. As for whose troops these were, for a city like The Hague the results would be catastrophic either way. Nor could I be joyful at this turn of events on my own account: despite my hitherto abundant experience in turning myself into a Frenchman from a German, or a German from a Frenchman, as circumstances required, I still hoped, I know not why, that in The Hague I would not have to make use of this commonplace science. I quickly began to get dressed, listening attentively as I did: I began to suspect that this racket was being made by neither French nor Germans and that, furthermore, this was no armed squadron, because what kind of army would march anywhere while striking up such a frantic drumming, whistling, and ratcheting—only indeed if it were an army of madmen, or of sages whose experiences over the course of time had led them to tap the few remaining barrels, so they could turn themselves into madmen in that way. But if they were neither French nor German, then who were these demented souls terrifying the residents of this already frightened city so early in the morning with such a hellish ruckus? The carnival was moving farther on. By the time I had gotten myself together the noise had moved along somewhat, but—quickly forgetting my idleness of the previous days—I set off after it, and presently I too glimpsed the drumming, ratcheting procession. I can say that it was a colorful company, not at all fitting beneath that cloud-covered sky, amid the somber and timid houses. The players of a small theatrical troupe were passing through the city as if they had been cast up here from some forgotten carnival, and they were doing their best to drum up an audience for that afternoon's performance. One of them wore a blue golden-braided cloak, as if he were a notary in a court of law, another wore checked clown pants, but my attention was drawn chiefly to a man who marched by most adroitly on stilts, stepping forward in an improbably long woman's dress trimmed with silk tassels, the train of the dress dragging behind. All those nearby were celebrating, three or four small boys in black gowns danced around him, while not a muscle moved on his face, as if it were carved from wood. The infernal music was supplied by most of the members of the group, joined by a few lads chasing after them, clapping together pieces of wood or beating pots full of holes with canes. This could have been a great pleasure for the lads; there had been no cause for gaiety in The Hague or its environs for a very long time.

The mid-afternoon performance would be taking place on the square in front of the church named for Saint Jacob. When the public had gathered, strange music came from the drums, cymbals, ratchet, and recorder; it sounded different from when we had all first heard the troupe marching into the city. On the recorder, a drawn-out, plaintive melody was played, while the other instruments played in a tighter, quicker rhythm, though never leaving the recorder behind. The rhythm and melody did not entirely suit each other, and yet there was a connection between them, the kind of connection between the movement of a person growing more distant as he runs away and the sight of clouds drifting along the horizon; but whereas the person running away finally disappears into the horizon, these two different kinds of music, no matter how long one listened, did not merge together, and yet at the same time there was something inexplicitly archaic in their tones, as if designating the arrival of centuries past.

After a while, the music grew more subdued but did not completely die out. First the man wearing the blue gold-braided cloak stepped into the square, taking his place behind a dais. On the dais a folio of paper waited for him, a quill, and a bottle of ink. When he appeared, the spectators began to move, some trying to draw closer to this emblematic theater so as to see better. The "stage" was simply a wide black tarpaulin spread out on the ground in front of the church steps. A gangly, scrawny woman shoved her elbow into my back, pushing me forward, and suddenly I found myself in front of the actor costumed as a notary in a court of law. From the first he acquitted himself in his role most excellently. I stood close to him, and yet could neither read his face nor deduce anything of what was about to happen. He examined the objects arrayed on the dais, sharpened the quill with great expertise and adroitness, unhurriedly unfolded and smoothed out the folio of paper, and placed the ink bottle nearby to comfortably dip the quill into it. Then, like someone who is well aware that ever since the world has been the world, every act committed on the stage can in the end be nothing other than a heinous crime, he turned toward the church and waited, for he appeared certain there would be something to note down in his registry. The public—at least those standing closest to the stage—waited with him, and no one grew impatient, even though for entire minutes there was no sign of anything to which we might be witness. The people in the back were more clamorous, which was understandable because the whole hullabaloo had not promised such a sequel as this. From them ever more agitated words were heard, ever louder whistling, which in no way disturbed the notary standing by the dais: he didn't even squint in the direction of the noise. This, however, only intensified their dissatisfaction: the conduct of such individuals is no doubt the same in every theater: they clamor for burlesque, the burlesque of the world at any price, and if they don't get it quickly enough, any actor or fastidious public of the boxes—who love to brood over the misfortune of the world and the people within it—would be well advised to stay out of their way.

The notary might have known this too, for with one arch of his eyebrow, which only the spectators standing close to him could see, the three little black-robed boys, the ones we had seen earlier at noon, jumped out from behind the church. They were now like three little devils from a folktale, their faces smeared with black. Turning somersaults, scrapping with each other, they rolled onto the stage, as if summoned here by a black hole, as if they were fox cubs poking their snouts into the light of day for the first time. When they took notice of us watching them, they looked frightened, and immediately left their squabbling, which it appeared had broken out over a cane, and which—in that dark hell pit that had led them here—might have been of particular value. The devil's children, in their fright, now hid behind one another, as if the light were damaging to them. Their mantles were too large, impeding their movements; they incessantly tripped over them, although they could pull the hoods low over their eyes. Of course, not contented with that, they clung to one another, the black devil's ball of their mass rolled to the edge of the tarpaulin, and the clutching once again became pushing and wrangling, once again the devil's children were completely immersed in their play. They did not notice when the notary of the court of law stepped out from behind his dais, carrying three sacks onto the stage, and took the cane for himself—that very cane for which these devil's children were getting ready to bloody each other's noses. And with one swish of the cane their quarreling came to a halt, the three devil's children somersaulted to three different points on the stage, and they sat up, gazing around in wonderment, as if only now they were truly seeing one another, and as if now they were only looking around at the world for the first time.

Presently they noticed the sacks. Competing with one another, one rolling, the other walking on all fours, the third gamboling like a billy goat, they straightaway went over to the sacks, and they had no doubt whatsoever that they had come across a game especially for them. They untied the mouths of the sacks, and the sacks began to speak, with the kind of words that one might expect from a dark sack. These were dark words, truly dark, and yet it was as if the devil's children were deaf, noticing nothing of what was happening to them through the notary's volition. From the first sack, amid loud guffaws, they pulled out a puppet, indescribably hideous, with swollen eyes and a crooked nose, on its head a pointed miter, then immediately from the second sack they pulled out a scholar puppet, all sorts of gobbledygook scrawled on its skull. Who were these puppets for? The devil's children, not bothering with the third sack, made the first two dance, spin around, leap, and jump ever more madly, and all the while an unknown, singing language poured out of them, as if it were the language of the puppets, as if it were their tongue, or rather that of the sacks: *Babel Babel abba bolal Babel Babel abba bolal kol kol kol.*

The devil's children danced and yelled, and the sacks kept on talking, and those of us standing there saw all of it, we heard all of it. There were those whose legs or bodies began to move involuntarily, drumming out the rhythm on the ground, while others beat their thighs; there were those who gazed, shuddering at what these devil's children were doing on the stage. The notary registered everything precisely. The quill in his hand never stopped, he furrowed the folio of paper, dipping his quill into the ink and writing; as the devil's children danced, he wrote. Then once again he raised the cane, once again it swished through the air, and from behind the back of the church a girl stepped out, wrapped in a large scarf. She lifted her dainty head from the scarf like the bell-shaped bloom at the end of the stalk of a lily of the valley. She approached the theater as if she were being led there, every gaze turned toward her, and suddenly this improvised little theater with its notary, its devil's children—and with us, the spectators—became something like the belly of a monster preparing to swallow all creation. Everything became mute. On the girl's face was a quiet smile of wonderment, but somehow the smile was also empty, as if it were speaking not to this moment but to the great emptiness of the moment immediately before the Beginning. And then, when the girl stepped onto the stage, my God, in this moment it was as if I were plunging into an unfathomable abyss, because I recognized who it was. It was Carlita, it was Carlita who was stepping onto the stage. How had she ended up here? What had she to do with this company? I looked only at her, I sensed only her. Her steps were heavy, as if it were not only her legs that she had to lift but the earth itself, the earth which indomitably clung to the soles of her feet. As she stood there, the scarf slid down to her silk mantle. Once again I established that I had not been mistaken when, arriving at the house of Signor del Filato with my captain, I had seen her as a kind of girl child and treated her as a desirable but not yet ripened fruit. Now, however, I ranged my gaze all over her, as men tend to do with women in possession of all the strength of their sex. To seize and plunder, it appears that this is what we want in the very last moment as well. I realized that I was not capable of understanding what was playing out before my eyes. For that, I would have to see everything again, everything would have to be repeated again, as in a dream. Carlita's face, her blind eyes were frightening. It was as if she had glimpsed, on the other side of darkness, the fallen trees of Paradise, the untraversable wastelands behind the veil of the luxuriant, fleeting world. But why, why had she come to this theater? The notary barely glanced up from his folio; he set the devil's children, who began to yelp like wild dogs, on her, as they grabbed again and again at Carlita's thighs, at her breasts, and all the while Carlita didn't move, as if she didn't even notice what was going on.

And then suddenly the devil's children seized her. It was a hideous spectacle. They seized her, pinned her to the ground, and with the two puppets—the one with the pointy miter on his head, and the one with the bulging eyes and the crooked nose—they executed diving somersaults in between Carlita's ever more stiffened legs, pointing toward the sky. I moved, perhaps I even took a step toward the theater, so as to bring an end to this atrocity. But the notary noticed my intention, raised his cane, and ordered me back with a single glance. From that point on, I watched the devil's children jumping, which didn't want to come to an end, as if in a stupor, I heard their ecstatic mutterings, their baying, and the clapping to an ever quicker beat, in a stupor, as they urged each other on. I have no idea what the others around me were doing, if they had fallen into a similar stupor, for I could imagine that they were pleased by what they saw.

While the devil's children were throwing Carlita to the ground, faint violin music had been filtering in from somewhere, a divinely beautiful slow music, an insane contrast to what was happening on the stage. After a while the music began to get louder, but now I heard only the voice of the violin, I no longer heard the yelps and the clapping of the devil's children, and in my horrified wonderment I watched as it seemed the devil's children in their black coats were flying around with their horrific puppets like trapeze artists, and Carlita's legs, pointed toward the sky, formed a kind of gate which opened up willingly before them.

When the music died down, the devil's children, with the truly gracious movements of circus performers, lifted Carlita up from the ground, as if they were helping a circus rider down from her horse, and Carlita then walked all across the front of the stage, as if she were counting on the recognition of the public after a magnificent circus act. I felt as though this mockery were directed personally at me; I didn't know what I had done to deserve it. It was as if I had hurtled down into an abyss. At the next gesture of the notary, one of the devil's children pulled out from the third sack a bridal gown, although it could be seen that this would not be its final use, as in many spots it had already turned yellow and was moth-eaten. This bridal gown was now placed upon Carlita; the best man stepped onto the stage on his stilts, in his hands was the violin, and it was as if he were no longer playing on that same refined instrument from which a moment ago such delicate sounds had crept out, but a worthless reed fiddle, with the wedding chords echoing falsely, insultingly from higher up.

I saw as they gave Carlita to the two puppets. The notary was the priest; she was led before him with the two puppets. Everyone was silent. The notary raised his cane, and holding it up in the air, with slow movements, drawing a cross, he blessed everyone who came in front of him. In nomine Patris et Filii et Spiritus Sancti. Carlita took the puppets, hugged them to herself, and, embracing them, withdrew from the theater in the direction from which she had come, along the side of the church of Saint Jacob. Before she disappeared, she was accompanied by the nuptial song of the devil's children, now rendered without a single false note:

It's pig-slaughter day, the knife, whirling, shines,
its blade whetted by the dawn wind,
the mantles are growing stiff in the air,
standing round the beast's body, so do the men.

The nooses are drawn tighter and tighter,
The mouths are foaming—the tongues are stiff.
The neighbor brings salt, he brings black pepper,
Time now to measure the victim's weight.

People say the dead here are lighter
than the living, in whom the blood is known:
they fight on the scales harder than life,
their weight, exaggerated, gives no sign.

Avoid the dogs with their burning muzzles,
and the vile man who drinks fresh blood,
until the shadows rise across the dark puddles
to the unclaimed goods of the beyond.

The devil's children sang as if they were pupils declaiming the most mischievous of love songs: for them it only consisted of ingratiating and cheerful allusions. As they reached the last bar, namely, "the unclaimed goods of the beyond," my senses became clear again: I could hear and see the people standing around me. The scrawny, gangly woman, who half an hour earlier had shoved me toward the notary of the court of law by digging her elbow into my back, was now practically falling down with laughter, and I saw that the others as well could hardly hold themselves back. I was obliged to conjecture that the events that had taken place on this improvised stage had been, from first to last, a magnificent amusement for all the others. This was even more the case as, accompanying the ratchets and drumrolls, resounding once again, a general mirth took hold of everyone, a mirth badly needed in this overcast little town. In this whirlwind danced the performers of the traveling circus, the blue cloak with golden braid appeared amid the revelers, the clown pants, the black mantles of the devil's children, and in the exact center of this merry ecclesia the man on stilts. I was incapable of fighting my way through the crowd. As if they had crept out from somewhere beneath the ground, once again here were the lads with their pieces of wood as they clapped them together, beating pots with holes in them with their canes, linking their arms with mine here and there.

"Get away!"—I tore myself away from their arms. "Get away because I don't know what I'll do to you!"—I had to find Carlita, perhaps only so that she could give me an explanation as to what had happened just now on the stage.

9
Concealed Map

Find Carlita on the streets of The Hague? Impossible. This was her city, which she knew blindfolded, whereas I, what was I here? A stranger, who eventually would no longer be able to say where he came from, a widow's son tossed by the wind to faraway lands. And my poor mother, what could she be thinking, wondering if I still lived. It had been a long time since I had conveyed any message to her; for a long time she hadn't entered my thoughts. My younger sisters certainly must have gotten married by now, and if they had not succeeded in catching a rich man—because, well, a fat fish does not land very often in the kind of torn net they would have been casting out—still, they must be getting along somehow, and perhaps had apportioned something to my mother, if nothing but an abundant cacophony of children. And as for me, what could I say about myself? Well, I had learned a few things and seen a few others. Namely, in my own insignificance, I was still standing right at the beginning, assuming that anything that seethes beneath the fur-belowed sky has a beginning. And as, it appears, sooner or later there arises in everyone the desire to see in advance—although still too soon, no doubt—what place they might occupy in this world so as to enclose themselves within a final, irrevocable framework, the idea began to arise in me that it was high time for me to go home and assume the position of surgeon in a small Swabian hamlet somewhere. This thought did not fill me with enthusiasm, but neither did it give rise to bitterness. Sooner or later the war would come to an end, the guard of the donjon, who sounded his bugle whenever troops were approaching the city, would soon be trumpeting the news of peace far and wide—which of course would mean simply that the weapons would be oiled, laid upon bits of straw, and locked up in wooden chests for a brief period of time. That day, however, had not yet arrived. And my feelings had been taken prisoner by Carlita, as if her disappearance were a message for me, just me.

Thus, while I tried to escape from the arms yanking me back into the swirling vortex of dancers, I myself became so agitated that I gave up trying to register any direction; I lost all sense of orientation. I entrusted myself fully to my intuition, as if Carlita—just like my younger sisters in childhood—were playing blind man's bluff with me: they would hide an apple in a corner of the house, and I had to search as they yelled out "cold" or "hot." But the arrangement of our house, the location of the furniture and staircase, were all inscribed into my senses, and I knew even with closed eyes exactly where I was. In The Hague I had already gotten lost with my eyes wide open. And my sole chance of seeking guidance was in observing what the city showed me on this or that street corner, what it offered to my eyes, knowing full well that Carlita never oriented herself according to such sights. Pictures, once again pictures, conveyed their messages to me:

In one of the upper windows of a three-story house, a woman was watering flowers, the water dripping onto the pavement below as if it were raining.

Behind a church, at the end of a short street that widened out like a sack, consisting of only a few houses, two boys were playing. One of the boys sat in a wooden-wheeled wheelbarrow, the other grabbed the handles of the wheelbarrow and ran with it, suddenly changing direction, turning here and there, trying to make his companion, who really had to hold on, fall out. Both of them were laughing; the game amused them greatly.

In front of a tavern, two men were unloading heavy beer barrels. They lowered them from the horse-drawn cart, then steered them over to a chute and rolled them down into a cellar, each time yelling out, "Ro-oll-ling!" In the cellar, the barrels must have been falling on a bed of thick straw; there must have been someone down there to move them farther on. The men lowered the barrels, steering them toward the chute, and they kept yelling out, "Ro-oll-ling!" There was a feed bag attached to the horse's head, and it ate from that.

And there were empty pictures too. Pictures in which nothing happened. There was no movement in them. And yet these too were also full. They were full of motionless things: gates, walls, edges and angles, absences that could not be precisely located, absences which could be filled at any time by a person, an animal, an object appearing suddenly—and there was some kind of light upon them, a light that showed everything.

By the time I got back to the house of Signor del Filato, it was evening. I did not meet up with my host, although I heard his steps; the wooden stair creaked familiarly as I closed the door behind me. I kept seeing in my mind's eye the theatrical scenes that had played out in front of the church of Saint Jacob, and now it seemed as if the notary of the court of law were beckoning to me with his eyebrows, indicating that I was next, now it was my turn. Just as I had that morning, I crouched by the edge of the bed with a woolen blanket thrown over my back: there was hardly anything left to heat with, everyone had to be sparing; during the day a fire could burn in the stove at most for half an hour.

It is difficult for me to convey the events of the following evening. I woke up several times, but without completely regaining consciousness from my harried dreams, whose backdrop was not The Hague—and yet had I not been in The Hague, I would not have gotten so wound up. Whether these were several dreams or just one dream repeating itself—continuing after the pauses of a wakeful stupor—I don't know; by morning nothing remained of them save one oppressive memory: I felt that certainly now a final awakening was approaching, as if something were alighting upon my face, and no matter how much I wanted to, I could not move my hand to drive it away. It was late morning by the time I woke up. The dull sunlight barely filtered in through the window, leaving me with no desire to rise, and as I looked at the washbasin awaiting me on the three-legged chair beyond the window, and thought of the freezing temperature of the water I would have to pour from the jug into the washbasin, I pulled the cover all the way up to my chin to steal a bit more time. My experiences of the previous day were deeply merged with the dark impressions of my nighttime dreams, which themselves had been able to slip into the gates of consciousness only because the guard had fallen asleep.

As I turned my head to one side to sink deeper into my pillow, I noticed a piece of paper on it. It was a missive, penned with pleasing golden letters, and as much air between the lines as was necessary. Curiosity gained the upper hand over exhaustion—as did fear, because I was certain that according to my habit I had locked the door to my room the previous evening. The letter read: "Esteemed Sir! The conspicuous interest with which You honored our performance of yesterday has emboldened me—if even in such a dubious manner, as if this letter, like a butterfly, had fluttered into Your room while You slept—to invite You this evening to . . ." (here an address followed, with a short description of how to get to the place), " . . . in a word, I should wish to invite You to a certain house, where, if I am not mistaken, a surprise intended especially for You shall be waiting. I should be immensely grateful if You would deign to come and if I might, in addition, beg Your forgiveness for not revealing how this letter happened to appear on Your pillow." The signature beneath the letter was so intricate and hastily scrawled that no matter how hard I tried, I could not decipher it, while the letter itself, as I have said, had been written without haste and in a clear, practiced hand. I only mention this because the signature, if I was indeed deciphering it well—a task which was approximately as simple as locating the seed-brimming sheath of a pea plant amid abundant weeds—began with a C, but I could not bring myself to believe that Carlita might have been the writer of the letter, despite her many peculiar abilities; and yet I was sure the surprise promised to me in the letter was connected to her.

Thus I waited impatiently all day for evening to arrive, so I could finally set off on the designated route and come to the place the letter had ordered me to go. It was not difficult to find the house. It stood on a small square near the Mauritshuis, not too far from where I had glimpsed the boys playing in the wheelbarrow and the beer-laden horse cart of the previous day. The little square was lined with bourgeois houses of three or four stories, and in reality they almost completely closed off the square, from which only two streets led out; one of them, upon which I approached the square following the directions I'd been given, led to the town hall; the other, facing opposite, led to the harbor. Altogether it was something like a stage, and it would have been even more so if there had been not only windows but balconies and loggias looking out on the square; buildings like that, though, were quite uncommon in The Hague. The houses here were built by industrious and honorable burghers to whose minds, especially during these wretched wartime years, the thought of making life into theater never would have occurred. Even so, where were those gentlemen who truly had something to hide, where were the treasures brought back from Spain, and where was John Maurice, prince of Nassau-Siegen, who became governor of Brazil and docked at the Delft harbor a few years later, bringing back riches as were never seen before in Holland! But those times had passed. The good burghers of The Hague never hung cunning curtains in their windows behind which one could imagine the existence of secrets. Although they too merely wanted to play their roles well, they found ever less joy in changes of clothes, their women had never really known the finer arts of allurement, or if they had ever known them, they certainly had reason to fear them; or they had good reason to button up their dresses all the way to the neck lest the promise of love slip in beneath their garments. If a lock of hair happened to peek out from beneath their crisp white linen caps, they immediately pushed it back. And their houses were just as lacking in ornament. Their unplastered brick walls, with their crimson color of fired clay and large windows, modesty emanating even from the slant of their roofs, seemed to inform all passersby: If it is a coulisse for games of temptation and deception you seek, then go south, go south until the sun begins to scorch the nape of your neck, for here everything must proceed with honor and candidness; because if not—if, in anyone, this wise order of unadorned daily life should break down—then there would be, liberated among these walls, forces so dark and so ruinous, of which those people down south, in the midst of their charming play, would never be able to conceive.

The house into which I stepped following the directions of the letter did not open on to the square but was accessed from a vaulted passageway which I noticed only at the last minute; immersed in my thoughts, I nearly walked right past it. The dark passageway with its crimson stone steps leading up to the house struck me as familiar; suddenly I had the distinct impression that I had been here once before. The marbled crimson of the steps, the erosion of the edges, the cracks, the small pockmarks in the stone, the pattern of darker and lighter splotches—it was as if I had seen all these before, had once before trod upon these very steps. At the landing, I rested for a moment. From above, light filtered out from behind a door. The same kind of vaulted corridor I had traversed coming in from the street led there, and it was just as low: if I reached up, I could touch the ceiling, white-washed with limestone, with the tips of my fingers.

I perceived no sign of movement in the house, I heard no sound, apart from that of my own steps, of course, no matter how noiselessly I tried to walk. The windows of the corridor opened on to the dark square. The good burghers of The Hague, I thought, were at that hour of the evening spooning the hot fish soup into their mouths at home with their own tranquil certitude, or were pouring their dreary yogurt into themselves, crumbling pieces of equally dreary black bread into it; the good burghers of The Hague were never tortured by any doubt beneath the wide heavens that they had not already done everything they could possibly do for the happiness of their fellow human beings. On such tranquil evenings as these, only a little light filtered out to the street from the taverns, somewhat more noisily though, because inside the glasses circulated zealously. The devotion surrounding the steins of beer consecrates the day that has passed, and the good kinsmen of The Hague could do no better than that, because if the passing day had been so merciful as not to have flung the earth away from the corners of their fields—although they all knew it was what they deserved—such a consecration was in order.

I too would have been happy to drink a stein of Tripel beer from the Carmelites, which, whether pale or dark, is more than ample for a person with no bread to eat, and furthermore, it will make you admirably tipsy. The house that stood behind the Mauritshuis was yet to release me, however. The room into which the vaulted corridor opened was completely empty. That is to say, it was not completely empty because next to the wall a candle blazed: a tall, thick candle, almost as high as a candle placed next to a catafalque. This didn't come to mind at the time, only now when I think back upon my last day in The Hague, because I know, my dear reader, what you don't—I know what happened in this house. If the candle had not been set there at the base of the wall, I would have had to grope in perfect darkness, thus I could have taken it as a sign of attentiveness, although I had no idea who might have placed it there, namely, who had summoned me, who awaited me in that house, and what the surprise promised me in the letter was—which, as I thought, must have some connection to Carlita.

The room was as low-ceilinged as the corridor had been. I nearly felt the ceiling pressing down on me. With the candle now in hand, I tried to find a way forward, my curiosity not allowing me to turn back; here, however, as the minutes passed by, I felt more and more as if I had been led into a wretched trap. All around me were windowless walls: there was only a kind of niche-like recess, a narrow arch pressed into the surface of the wall about one hand's-width deep, which might have been a window at one time, but if it had been, the owner of the house had walled it up, who knew why. I no longer had any doubt: I had truly walked into a trap. Candle in hand, casting uncertain clouds of light on the walls and the low ceiling, I paced the room for some minutes at a loss. It had already occurred to me that the letter of that morning was nothing more than a bitter prank in which Carlita unequivocally had taken part. For some reason she wanted to make me ridiculous, and, so it seemed, she had succeeded. I would not have been surprised if she and her companions, the inventors of the theatrical piece of the previous day, had leapt out from the corridor with cries of shrill laughter. I took a step in that direction, as if wishing to overtake them, and yet still I turned back, and holding the candle slightly higher looked around again. I then noticed that there was a door built into the wall facing the niche-like recess. I didn't understand how this could have escaped my attention before. The door opened from this low and narrow room into a room that was splendidly illuminated. It was a magnificent hall, at least forty steps long and perhaps twenty steps wide, nearly big enough for the giving of balls, I would say, if the previous narrow little room that led here had not made it seem quite improbable that balls would have been given here, even in the prewar years of plenty—or if they had been, they would have been most peculiar balls, not the kind which could be imagined by one such as myself.

As I stepped into the hall and straightened up, I grew dizzy from its dimensions, not so much its length but its height. I felt that the other small room had succeeded in pressing down on me, and now I stepped into the larger hall almost as a Lilliputian. The builder, or whoever it was who had undertaken this commission, clearly had intended for very small people to step in here, people who would not be able to forget their smallness for a single moment, nor would they be able to forget the dizziness that seized them on entering this hall. And even after taking a few steps into the room, they wouldn't be able to grow used to it, not even when their eyes had adjusted to the height of the ceiling.

It was as if the builder of this house were saying, Do not forget that you are not the measure of things: it is not you who are the measurer but you who are being measured. The place where you are is measuring you right now. Because it was as if he had built the ceiling twice as high and the ceiling of the previous room so low that you had to move through it on all fours. And he knew how to work with light, too. The torches affixed high up beneath the ceiling illuminated the walls sharply, while the light flowed beneath them like honey, and everything below remained in half-obscurity, so it was necessary to withdraw to the base of the wall and look up to see anything at all.

And those walls, my dear God, those walls! The entire hall was painted all round with pictures, and yet in such a refined fashion that it was as if silk, not paint, were covering the wall. I pulled my fingers along its surface, I kept touching it, ran the palm of my hand over it, even sniffed it. It was truly as fine as silk. It was weightless and thick; it lived and breathed. Perhaps it was the honeylike light filtering down that made it seem that way, or the meeting of the two kinds of light, for in my hand I still carried the candle I had found in the previous room. But I don't think so, for when I closed my eyes, entrusting myself completely to the sense of touch, I touched the faces and the hands, for surely these were people painted on the walls: they were covered with genuine skin, living material. My groping slowly grew keener. I felt, or at least I believed that my fingers were touching the hair's-width wrinkles of skin, its tiny craters, the running of its veins, its protrusions and scars. River valleys, precipices, inlets, mountains. This was a human map, covered by the silk of clothes, weightless and thick. So this is what the body is like for a painter! A concealed map, a throbbing surface. Whereas I, who tortured bodies with knives, forceps, saws, and drills, opening up skulls, chopping off limbs, slicing open veins—well, and of course I sewed, I always sewed, never thinking of the skin, always just thinking of what lay beneath it, the torn flesh, the broken bones.

And who were these people who were painted on the walls? Despite the half-light, I recognized them. Sitting next to a table, immersed in conversation, sat my host and Master Cottem, while Véronique served them fish with dill. The honeylike dark light flowed and flowed beneath. In the next scene, Véronique was pictured on her deathbed. Her face was like a puppet's, tortured and yet somehow still happy. Then came the picture of a burning city and Carlita's blind gaze. The room was like a picture book. It was Noah's Ark, onto which the last living beings had escaped, where Noah had saved their memories. I touched every picture with my hand, I caressed all of them with my fingers. I was overcome by dizziness, the same dizziness I had felt when I first stepped into the room. The next picture once again showed Carlita as she slept amid the sand dunes. The picture was dark; only a little light was cast upon Carlita's face, but in such a way as if crystal grains of sand were pouring down on it. You wanted most of all to wake her up, before the break of dawn, before the sky began to glimmer, when her face would be completely buried within the sands. But whoever painted her wanted her to keep on sleeping, although it was clear that her slumber was anything but restful. A tiny muscle convulsed in the corner of her mouth, betraying her dread, the dread on her childlike face, but it was not possible to see into the depths of her dreams—for here there were only maps and surfaces.

In one scene I was pictured too. It portrayed the story I had related to Signor del Filato on one of my first evenings in his house in order to win his confidence and to get him to tell me some stories, too. "These sorts of things are handled much better in France," I began the story, but my host clearly saw through me, perhaps enjoying the tale anyway, although he knew that I had been neither to Calais nor to Paris, just as I had no luck with that lady from Brussels, to whom, for the sake of the story, I had introduced myself as Monsieur Buisson. And yet the scene had been painted; this story too had ended up on Noah's Ark.

After having introduced myself, I inquired of the lady if she had come from Paris. No: she was going that route, she said.

Well, then, such a lovely lady as yourself could not reside anywhere but London.

At this, a fine smile appeared on the lady's face, and perhaps she even blushed a bit, and she indicated with a slight motion of her head that she was not from London.

Then Madame must have come from Flanders.

From there, my lord, she answered.

And then I provided her with a list of names of cities, Arras, Cambray, and Ghent, until I finally gave her the gift of the name of Brussels, like a genuine pearl among the false, although it was no different from the other cities I had passed through, a nest of boredom and misery, only ornamented after a fashion by imagination. But imagination, which at one time created continents, the lower and upper worlds echoing with laughter, now stumbles, shortsighted, into that narrow, dark, and mute dominion where it is enclosed by temperance. This is why the touch of every living thing is so dead and cold. Signor del Filato might have known this too, and that is why he had painted not only poor Véronique, himself, and Carlita but the figures of his other pictures, including myself, as if these bodies beneath the living skin had all long since been dead. As to the fact that he was the painter who had worked in this room, I no longer had the slightest doubt. The bodies now withdrew back into the walls, and from there their skin, the maplike surface, became chilled.

Dead shores, continents, oceans. I could make contact with the feelings and thoughts of Signor del Filato as little as I could touch the bodies now retreating back into the walls, but now, in this room, where I felt myself to be so small, I somehow entered into their proximity. The next picture was the same as the first: Master Cottem and my host sat at a table immersed in conversation, while Véronique served them with fish with dill. In this picture, however, which filled about a third of the wall, more obscurely lit, across from the door, the place of Master Cottem was taken by Signor del Filato, while I sat in the latter's place. I raised the candle, and slowly passed in front of the picture, returning to this or that individual detail so nothing would escape my attention. I hoped that I might find an answer in this picture as to why, even if unwillingly, I had become a part of the household of Signor del Filato, and perhaps I could also discover what had happened to Carlita.

Even today I do not know if I understood correctly what

I was seeing. And so I entrust this judgment to you, my dear reader; I beg you be the judge of this matter, if you so wish. This painting repeated the mise en scène of the first, in which Master Cottem sat at the head of the table. Before him on the table rested a sketch, but what it depicted could not be discerned. The finger of Master Cottem pointed at a certain spot on the sketch, while he himself looked at my host expectantly. From the bearing of Signor del Filato, it could be seen that a mere moment ago he had been leaning over the sketch with strained attention, but now, as the painting was finished, his gaze had turned toward Véronique, just then stepping into it, his countenance, now milder, bearing the signs of love. This mildness, of course, could also have been intended for the lovely piece of fragrant fish which Véronique carried in, holding it ceremoniously in front of her on a wooden platter. The warm intimacy of this family scene received its reply, like a kind of apocalyptic premonition, in the scorched eyes of the fish, sweeping the figures in the picture, themselves unknowing, to the edge of destruction.

The next picture in front of which I now stood, my candle held high, repeated this scene, but with other figures, namely, Carlita and myself. These dinners, with their company of three, must have given rise to old, and with the passage of years ever more painful, memories in Signor del Filato. And yet my appearance at his house might have caused a certain kind of slippage, arising from both the past and the future, in his memories—his memories which I never knew, and of which I shall never know any more than what I have related to you, my dear reader. For instance, I could have perceived that Signor del Filato was worried about Carlita, about what would happen to her if he died. I did not, however, suspect my host's inclusion of me in his plans, perhaps in order to overcome his premonitions of the previous picture.

In this picture, instead of a sketch an open book lay upon the table. Signor del Filato pointed at something within it; his gesture was the same as Master Cottem's had been— clearly he was pointing at a word, which, of course, could not be read. And on the lengthened, age-withered face of my host was a similar look of expectancy as he gazed at me, and yet it was completely different from the look of expectancy on the face of Master Cottem. What he read in the book terrified him; he was overcome with the kind of dread as when someone comes face to face with an old terror. It was not consolation that he needed, or explanations; he wanted proof that what he saw was not true. I, however, was not leaning over the book, and I took no notice of my host's fear. My entire body was turned toward Carlita, who stepped toward the table just like Véronique in the previous picture, ceremoniously holding the wooden platter before her, upon it the roast fish. Yet in this picture the head of the fish had been cut off. On the wooden platter lay only the body of the fish, garnished with fresh dill leaves. But its eyes—the eyes of the fish remained in the picture. Carlita looked at her father with eyes that were as empty and frightening as those of the fish; in front of Signor del Filato was a knife for slicing it.

Holding the candle in front of me, I stood before the picture for a long time. With my fingers, I traversed all its regions, its chill surfaces, as if the tips of my fingers were discovering the true and imagined regions of all the years of my wandering, now lost. Pain shot through my loins for having never truly gained possession of this body. It was a farewell—a murder. Carlita's face inscribed itself within me, a perfect replica was created, a replica which time could no more destroy than the sandy dunes of the ocean shore, the ocean itself, the water's undulations. That evening I left The Hague.

10

The Beautiful Harmonies of Ruin

In the old book dealer's shop where I stop by from time to time, there once turned up in my hands a book by an eighteenth-century German writer, printed in Gothic lettering. It wasn't a first edition; a book like that can't be pulled down from the shelf so casually. Instead, it must be fought over at auction with other collectors as if waging a duel in which, even before the first bid, anyone to whom its acquisition is not the fulfillment of fateful coherence, the rebirth of the book itself, is doomed to failure. That wasn't my reason, though, for stopping by the secondhand book dealer's: for me, fate is a mesh, unraveling, knitted back up again and again; no, I went there for the dusty fragrance of the books, the yellowed pages, the battered book covers—in other words, for that bit of free time of which I deprived no one, but with which I bestowed upon myself a perfect, idle tranquillity, for I knew that in the secondhand book dealer's nothing would ever happen, just as nothing ever happened in the picture which hung on the wall across from my bed in my childhood. The secondhand book dealer's was a painted theater in which it was not young ladies and young lords who stepped onto the stage but writers: one burdened by care, the next with a countenance both merry and dour, and all sorts of players in this clamorous, vortex-like market, where it was not possible to acquire the usual sorts of goods, or delicacies favored by gourmets, but instead that most precious of merchandise—the variegated assortment of all that is fleeting. That is why I felt no need to purchase any of the books I perused there. It was enough for me to smell them: the scent of deterioration, of things passing, filled me with pleasure. Of course I dipped into parts of this or that book, why wouldn't I have, and from time to time, and after long pondering, the idea of purchasing one did come into my mind, but, I must add, only in the case of books from which I did not detect that vortex-like commotion. For there are mute books as well. They are mute like the grave. In such books, the letters' grains of sand, beautifully formed into mounds by the pressure of the two hard covers, conceal the bodies—those of the characters and the writer's—before my eyes; and when one peruses their lines, it's as if the reader were wearily digging out those bodies to recite a prayer of mourning for them—a prayer which everyone deserves.

The secondhand book dealer's shop was located a few steps below street level. As I stepped in, the little bell above the door rang, and the secondhand bookseller, an elderly gray-faced bearded gentleman—you could never imagine him being anywhere else—nodded in my direction, not impeding me with speech but allowing me to take myself straight in between the shelves. The books, judiciously selected, awaited me in the eternally unchanging half-obscurity. I had seen the book dealer in the act of purchasing his wares countless times, and I can attest that he did not buy just anything. It was as if he were selecting them for himself. Among his books were certain volumes that sat on the shelf for months, and yet if someone should nonetheless take a book over to him to pay, he would from behind his desk nod approvingly, and, having written out the receipt, hand the book over like a reward which that customer fully deserved.

The autobiography of the eighteenth-century German writer, needless to say, had sat on the shelf for months now. I don't think that apart from myself anyone else's gaze had ever happened upon it, this edition from the beginning of the twentieth century. The tart scent of its thick yellow pages evoked many homes from the time before the war, now lost; such homes used to be crammed with such books. I myself had seen in an elegant flat in central Pest the remnants of such a home, rescued—or plundered—under who knew what conditions. And yet if we look back from a sufficient distance, we can see that to steal something means to save an object, for at least a small amount of time, from certain destruction. The top of the gigantic book cabinet, consisting of two parts, was reinforced by a triangular escutcheoned pediment, as if crowning a gate of victory. The baroque Venetian table with the six chairs placed around it, all spiraling legs, hoops, and decorative trims, was a memorial to the unknown life of a stranger, a life surrounded by mistakes, nostalgia, denial, and regret. In the presence of these old books, seeing these furnishings which seemed more antique than their actual age, I felt neither nostalgia nor regret. I had no reason to. What had passed had passed; I always thought this. In this world there is no greater benefactor than transience, because the bullet, which time sends off with a light, triumphant hand, forever misses its target. And that is why I loved the imagination enclosed within books, the single antidote to the existence of this world, the unexpected denouement of sentences, exchanging the distant for the near, then abruptly giving back what it had taken, thrusting it even closer than I would like, directly into the midst of my own life.

I had taken down the book of the eighteenth-century writer—for months it had aroused no one else's interest—from the shelf several times, holding it up to my nose and sniffing it before once again regretfully establishing that since it was printed with Gothic letters, it would certainly demand too much exertion on my part. My regret, however, became more and more pronounced, and the acidic scent of the book seemed to promise more and more, and of course the name of the author as well; I had read two of his other works in the meantime. And so the time came when I had no choice; I had to buy the book. The used-book dealer nodded in recognition, noting that he had been certain for a long time that this volume would be mine. After I brought it home, I didn't begin reading it right away. I picked it up only weeks later, always with a certain reserve, because of those Gothic letters. But my reserve soon passed. I got used to the letters, and in exchange for the difficulties of the beginning, I came across superb details concerning the writer's childhood. A German childhood, around 1730. A tiny microcosm, overflowing with ominous fears, thoughts both repressed and more lucid than the brightest light.

One of the incidents described in the book touched me closely. The writer might have been thirteen or fourteen years old, an apprentice soldier, when his father died. After the funeral, the more immediate relatives accompanied the widow and her only son back to the house. Along with the great-aunts, the silent, younger aunt of the writer, Annerl, then about twenty years old, also came. Annerl's teeth stood out a little: they were snow white, and beautiful, and when she laughed they glittered splendidly, and one was obliged to consider—our writer narrates in his characteristic style— whether she was also laughing in order to show them off. Her smile was made even more alluring by the way her teeth jutted out slightly, emphasizing the harmony between face and figure, seasoning her beauty and grace. Our writer denies that the word *love* would be fitting here. He was fond of his aunt: ever since he'd been a small child, he'd found joy in looking at her. He would sit next to her for hours while she embroidered, not a muscle moving on his face.

After the funeral, the family sat down together in the house; after a while the writer's mother and great-aunts went to the inner room, and he was left alone with Annerl. They didn't move as they sat next to each other, remaining silent on the divan. The funeral had made them both unaccustomedly exhausted. "How tired I am!" said Annerl, suppressing a yawn. She raised her right hand weakly, and with her white fingers she began to tap her own mouth, as if completing some kind of superstitious rite. "Are you tired too?" she asked her nephew.

While she said this, she laid her head on the boy's lap, who knows why, and remained that way, motionless. The trousers of my uniform—writes the older man, who had once been that boy, remembering the incident—trembled from the honor bestowed upon me: I could serve as Annerl's pillow. I was befuddled by the fragrance of her skin. I studied her profile as she rested there, her tired, bright eyes wide open. And, he says, that is all that happened. But he never forgot that feeling when, for a moment, that blissful weight rested upon his thigh. It was an extraordinary feeling of delight; he compares it to the feeling elicited by the weight of a medal of honor pinned upon one's chest.

The weight of a medal of honor pinned upon one's chest. I could read no farther in the book. My father at the time was already dead. I sat there on the edge of his bed, the bed from which he would no longer rise, and we had words for each other, inasmuch as he was able to speak through the stupor of tranquilizers; I knew I could not compensate for any omissions with these few days. But, well, what kind of omission could this have been? In those hours I didn't even try to overcome the repulsion, the ever-accumulating antipathy, the strange, numbing mixture of fear and desire, so easily mistakeable for hatred, that flared within me; I knew I truly had no words for the feelings that at once numbed me and filled me with tension, for repulsion, desire, fear, and hatred were but distant echoes of that pain that rendered me motionless up to my throat, the crown of my head. My father's hands were dry, and yet still powerful. His hand could not receive the warmth of my hand; it was a dead object, it rested in my lap lifelessly, just as the lovely head of Annerl rested on her nephew's thigh. Nothing could have happened. Death, that great benefactor whom we awaited, was late. I took my father's hand, I spoke to him; he indicated something with his eyes, or replied at times with one or two words. Then he whispered that sentence, painfully, thinking of my mother, for surely he always thought of her, he whispered that even a horse deserves to be caressed. I understood, I really understood this. And when, in the autobiography of the German writer, I got to the passage about his father's funeral, and I could see in my mind's eye as Annerl's green-blue eyes wearily became absorbed in the face of her nephew, as in the surface of a lake never furrowed by waves, suddenly I realized my gaze had been immersed in exactly the same way. I saw nothing else, only the creases of the white sheet covering my father's body like the quiet undulations of the water's surface. And I sat there with a faint smile above these white undulations, my face almost aching from it, and when I stood up from the side of the bed and turned away, my father's face fell away from me, gave itself over to the benefactor, to Death, who perhaps stepped forward in the form of a German peasant woman, or a girl resembling Annerl, with teeth that stuck endearingly out, and after my father had adjusted his uniform, ironed to a perfect crease, and of course with the medal of honor pinned to his chest, he took the arm of the young woman and strolled out of the wretched memory of this world.

Perhaps no one else had ever seen him, only the regent. But, his eyes bandaged, my father couldn't care less who was standing in front of him. In his ears the beautiful harmonies of ruin were already murmuring, the same harmonies the rabbi of Putnok, Salamon Widder's friend, had heard, whose sound nearly drove him mad. These sounds took my father into themselves as well. He stood at attention, his thighs trembled. The world swam before him in white beneath the bandages, just as white as the uniform of the rear admiral, just as white as another hospital bed later on, from which he never rose again. White were the walls of the sick ward, the window frames, the nightstand next to the bed, white were the nurses' uniforms as they glided behind the window someone had forgotten to close. This whiteness swallowed my father's face, his hands, his body—swallowed them into itself, sucking them into itself, destroying, devouring them.

He is not anywhere, he never was anywhere—it was not he who stood there watching the boat pulling out of the harbor at Hamburg, its low horn bellowing, it was not he who came home; that life spent with clenched teeth was not his, nor was it my mother's, nor was it mine—it was no one's, a wave that ran toward the shore, a wave that barely crested and now it is already smoothed out, ended, ended.

The skin on my father's hand was completely dry. I let it drop back onto the white sheet next to his body, I stood up, and I walked out of the hospital room. Before me was the long white corridor. Then the hospital park. It was morning; somebody was sweeping the fallen leaves next to the sidewalk. I was empty, at last I was completely empty. And it was with this emptiness that I took farewell of my father, not then and there, in the hospital park, but earlier, when he was still alive. I was beyond everything that was devastated within me, within him, within all of us, in everyone around us. This emptiness became filled with a life which I had to call my own. I got on the train, exactly there where my father, next to the wheel of the plundered railcar, had picked up a package. And the sweater which my mother had knitted from that snowflake-flecked yarn, the yarn she found in the package, traveled with me: it was in the suitcase on the rack above my head, it traveled the same route it must have taken in 1944. It was summer's end, morning, and even then the sun blazed in the windows flowing with streaks of rust. Bánréve, Putnok, Berente. The train jolted along with infinite slowness, staggering through the cornfields, frequently stopping in the middle of nowhere. Szentpéter, Keresztúr. The same roads, eternally the same, traversed by the living and the dead. I felt as if I would never reach my goal, as if I would never be free of them.

Pictures remain on the surface of oblivion, dark and menacing blotches. The high-ceilinged vaulted corridors of the dormitory with its windows overlooking the garden. The chill thick walls, the pale green of the wainscoting. Washing in the mornings, leaning, half-naked, over the troughs formed from tin sheets. The gleam of the emergency light above the door at night. The hours spent awake, listening to the whispering of the others, the noise of their slumber. The streets filled with November fog in that city where two years previously the gunshots had boomed out. Who saw then, and who dares to see today the thick black blood flowing in every direction on the basalt paving stones? The path leads downward along Déryné Street until it reaches a wide, crimson three-story building. Its arches devour the children's bodies, the faces and the years, and as for what it gives back, these are no longer bodies, no longer faces but the uniform costumes and masks of long-since motionless time.

In the dormitory, we girls would try on each other's clothes, we exchanged hair clips, we gave each other belts. At that time wide lacquered belts were the fashion, with big round buckles. We differed from one another in nothing, we easily could have exchanged our lives, just then beginning, as well. And right at that moment it was as if motionless time were beginning to surge, heaping its promises upon us. Every Sunday evening three or four of us would go to the movies, dancing, to the university club, or to the theater. We fantasized and we hoped. And all the while we never let go of each other's hands. We were something like Ági Balázs in

Rainy Sunday, and all the while we wished we could have been like brave Olga Bakonyi. Or at least a little bit like her. We sat in the dark while on the screen Olga Bakonyi showed off her legs, strolling around the pavement of the Sports Pool in Pest. The long calves, the ankles, and especially her feet, every one of her bones knew that she was beautiful. They had the courage to be beautiful. Yet we had learned that anyone who was too courageous could not be happy in the end. Happiness was quiet, that's what we learned. And Ági Balázs looked really happy as she sat on the steps of the National Museum next to the handsome new high school teacher, Pali Kászas. She let him put his arm around her shoulders. In the cinema, you could have heard the sound of a pin drop. It was a rainy Sunday afternoon. But I had never been to Pest in my entire life—that was a different country. *So good to hide away, so good.* There the streets were radiant, the girls were prettier, the air had a different fragrance. *This little solitude with you tempts me so.* Then one day, at the university club, something happened. I met my own Pali Kászas. He asked me to dance. And suddenly everything began to move within me, my thighs, my breast, as if they were carrying me away with themselves. He pulled me so close to him that I could hardly catch my breath. My skin was burning, my loins filled with blood. If he had let go of me while we were dancing, taking his arm from my waist, I would have slumped over like a rag doll. I laid my face upon his shoulder, and I let him take me wherever he wanted to across the dance floor. I consented to everything. I had no objections. Left leg steps, right leg steps. If at that point anyone had opened up my head, excising a nice little arc from my skull, they would not have seen demonic flames flaring up in the depths of gloomy desolation, but an empty horizon, and they would not have heard the crackling of flames, but instead would have listened intently into the broad silence, perhaps not even broken by the sounds of a heartbeat.

After that we began to meet. I told my girlfriends that I was in love, I was like a huge cannon, like a Bertha cannon, but in love, if such a thing could exist; you could have shot all of Miskolc to pieces with me. Poor dear old Alfred Krupp, who was pathologically terrified of fire, draughts, and intrigue—he never suspected what he had invented. In any event, it was not he who named the cannon after his wife, Bertha Eichhoff, who was twenty years younger than he, but the soldiers on the front, soldiers in whom the desire for a healthy life still glimmered. You're lucky, Berta, you don't even know how lucky you are. And in reality, I didn't know. And still I had my own ideas about happiness, even if they were taken from the movie screen or books: ideas about destruction, provocative desire whose fulfillment was the only excitement I wanted, and of course notions about faithfulness and possession. My God, what ideas I had! They were no better than those of Alfred Krupp, who in a speech to his workers—who were of course all men—said, "Enjoy what has been granted to you. After a day's work, stay among your loved ones, your parents, your wife and children, and reflect on the household and education. That ought to be your policy. However, save yourself the upset of high state politics. Conducting higher politics requires more time and insight into conditions than the worker has been granted." And if I think about it, in 1962 no one said, showed, or preached anything different to us, only of course now not only to the boys, but to the girls too, because the world had changed, yet still everyone had to know what the limits of their own politics could be. And nothing within me ever protested against this. I heard every word, but it was as if it was not being addressed to me, not to me, because what did I have to do with men, the old parents, housework; but whom else would they have been addressing, whom else would that finger be pointing at, saying: This should be your politics, and I never pushed away that pointing finger, not then or later on; I only wanted time, just a little bit of time, time that would last forever, as I was being led across the room by a series of dance steps. The music played, and within me was silence, I was as deaf as a veteran artilleryman.

My own Pali Kászas was the secretary of the Hungarian Communist Youth Organization of Miskolc University. His countenance was brightened by public concern and the consciousness of his own personal relevance. Following him were his hangers-on, boys and girls wreathed in cigarette smoke, the friends of my own Pali Kászas with whom I had nothing, but absolutely nothing, in common. Of course if we were alone, we too discussed politics, we debated, we too blew out the cigarette smoke. The Hungarian Communist Youth Organization advertised a country-wide campaign to increase the number of subscribers to the central newspaper *Hungarian Youth*. The number of new subscribers that had to be drummed up in Miskolc was given to us. Target figures, action groups, mobilization, even more organizing, even more cigarette smoke. There was no point to any of it. But even so I canvassed in the dormitory, how could I not have, even if they sneered at me for it? *Each tap of each raindrop telling a story, so good, so good to hide away,* I hummed to myself, and in the meantime I thought about my own Pali Kászas, just as if I were Ági Balázs.

And all at once I realized that there had been no one by my side for a long time. I heard from a mutual friend that my own Pali Kászas had been sent to Debrecen to serve in the Party Committee there. You didn't hear about it? How could I have heard about it? We hadn't broken up, but there was no more connection between us. Then, after Pali Kászas, there were more boys. One of them wrote poems; he pictured himself as a great poet, a kind of Attila József, whom he always referred to only by his first name, Attila—and if he wasn't a great poet yet, he certainly would be one day, if I, whom he had chosen as his muse, would be his unceasingly attentive and interested helpmeet. His poems were unpleasantly bad, filled with clumsy images, great suffering, and uncountable idiocies. But still a person spoke through them, as well as he could, and because he didn't have much language he betrayed much about himself about which he should have remained silent. If I had wanted to, I could have understood something about him, although if I had understood—who knew?— perhaps I would have loved him; in any event perhaps I would have lost my advantage in relation to him, something I didn't want: to fall in love and to succumb, to fall in love and be the weaker one, no, I didn't want that.

At the university afterward, there were smart, handsome boys with whom I could discuss literature, philosophy, history. We walked through the Great Forest in Debrecen, in the wintertime too, circling the lake several times, either in twosomes or with several others. We sat in the Palm Restaurant, we drank rum, humming along with the singer, a slightly hunchbacked boy, his fingers long and elegant like that of a pianist, we hummed melodies from Elvis Presley songs. Even today I can see how that boy raised his hand as he sang of love and tenderness, his palm open, up to the heights, his elegant pianist's fingers ascending, with closed eyes, and a deep, tempered voice. Someone mentioned the Elvis Presley film *Love Me Tender,* released ten days after the Soviet tanks rolled into Pest. The engine driver, deeply in love, looked into the eyes of Debra Paget, and the gaze of both of them was completely empty. Happy and empty.

The tanks rumbled in, and one of the boys put his arm around my shoulders. The tanks thundered along Bajcsy Zsilinszky Street, proceeding from Nyugati train station—the first one turned its gun barrel, and across from the Basilica it blew an apartment house to bits because a madman had shot a couple of rounds at the Russians with a drumfed machine gun from there. Happiness would follow us everywhere, sang Elvis. The boy who put his arm around my shoulders wanted to start kissing my neck. I allowed him to, but did not reciprocate, as if I hadn't even noticed. What film had he learned this gesture from? There was some film or another spinning around in all of us. Those rainy Sundays had come to an end within me a long time ago, and in all honesty, I had no desire to be Debra Paget. I had suddenly fallen out of all the love-me-tendering, I still saw how the singing boy raised his opened palm, I heard his voice too, deep and yet somehow lucidly delicate, I sensed the boys around me, sensed someone putting his arm around my hips, but I had nothing to do with any of this, I wasn't there, in a moment the Palm Restaurant had disappeared, the Great Forest had disappeared, because the mere thought was enough: no, I could never take home one of these lawyer's or doctor's sons from Debrecen, could never sit them down at the table next to my mother and father without giving my parents away, without giving away their own unhappiness, their crudeness, without them giving me cause for shame, even with a single word, a bad question or a crude joke, with everything—their bodies, movements, and smells, the objects that surrounded them.

I was at home, and I saw, on the top of the varnished chest of drawers, the heron carved from wood that my father had brought home from Hajdószoboszló, its white paint already worn off. Next to it I saw the bottle of apricot brandy, the shot glasses placed upside down. And in the glass-fronted cabinet, I saw pictures from the time my father was a policeman. I watched as my mother cleaned the parsley roots on the pale green sideboard, and I sensed that heavy smell in which was mixed the bodily odors of my mother and my father, the damp walls, food, and the chrysanthemums brought in from the garden with their large blooms, the chrysanthemums which always stood in a brown glass vase in the middle of the table.

I shouted out, No-o-o!—but only within myself, mutely. Already another tune was playing, the boy with the glasses and the slightly hunched back was singing another song about the change coming to our lives. And yet somewhere deep inside me I still loved those cemetery flowers! I loved that brown glass vase! And I loved the pale green credenza, I loved those heavy odors. Elvis sang of realizing our mistakes. What mistakes should be admitted, Elvis? Do mistakes even exist, and if they do, are these our mistakes? Do repulsion and attraction awaken within us, in our bodies, or do they awaken outside us, in the hand that signs the law, the finger which does not pull the trigger? Do devotion and hatred live within us or do they live in the objects, in the walls of our houses, in the clothes, in the gun barrel of a tank ready to fire, on the movie screen? Can we live out anything other than the hidden shame of our mothers and fathers? Can our most concealed feelings and thoughts, our bodies and our souls be anything other than a skein of yarn, woven—who knows since when—by invisible hands, then unraveled, and woven again until the threads grow thin and frayed and finally break?

Two weeks later, I traveled home to the village of my grandparents. There was a wedding, a spring wedding, in May, those are always the most beautiful. I didn't have to be there; the groom was a distant relative, and no one would have been offended had I not gone. But I had a sudden desire to see once again those blackened, moss-grown thatched roofs which the houses pull down over their eyes like the old women pull down their kerchiefs. In winter or fall, when the darkness settles down on the Bükk Mountains and retreats as far as the mountain ridge, one can easily get lost in time, one day passes just like another, but in Maytime the light seems to push the kerchiefs farther back on the women's heads, and each morning promises something, at least something that will help you hold out till noon or afternoon. On the night before the wedding, the entire village was busy with preparations: pastries were carried over to the bride's house. I arrived in the afternoon, staying with my uncle's family. The next day I went with his wife to the church, and from there across the brook to the bride's parents' house. The apple trees were already blooming in the gardens, the bed of the stream was full, leafy twigs carried along on its surface. I would have been happy to stay on the bridge, leaning across the banister and watching the current. For me, this village was something like a shell is to a snail. All the same, though, it had its faults. Later on, when I was ill, on the darkest days I felt my body was not covered by flesh and bones but a kind of mucus-like, slippery mass, itself enveloped by nothing. I pulled myself along its glittering secretion, and it was the most I could do to withdraw from the eyes of others, to disappear, to become invisible before anyone could speak to me or touch me. If I think on it well, my body never desired men. There was desire within me, but fear was greater. Every touch, even a simple peck on the cheek, left me both yielding and cold. Anyone could penetrate me with a word or an insult: they never encountered resistance, but they never found anything resembling a living person either. And as the years passed, I grew ever more stout. Maybe the illness began with that. I grew a soft husk around myself. After a while I put on weight even if I didn't eat anything. And I was there inside somewhere, in the depths of this husk, having contracted to a tiny size. There I lived untouched, within my own darkness. I needed someone who knew that, someone made from the same material as my own body, who would not feel the softness and coldness but only that which was good, only that which was strong, like the husk itself, and who, over the years, would slowly dissolve in this material, would become lost in it mutely, and between us there would be no reproaches.

When with the wife of my great-uncle I stepped off the bridge at the end where the road leads toward the mountain, three young people from the village were walking from the other direction. I had known all of them a long time, but I did not remember their names. I didn't look at them, turning my head away. They said hello, and the wife of my great-uncle returned their greeting. We walked beside each other, took a few more steps, and then I turned around. In the same moment the shortest of the young boys also turned around. That's all that happened, nothing more. There remained in my eyes a face, a pair of eyes staring into it. They were watery blue eyes, almost as white as the sky. They were transparent, like the brook. In other words they were dark, completely dark. And their halo was yellow. I asked the wife of my great-uncle if she knew who that was. If she knew the name of the shortest of the boys we had just passed. That evening I sought him out. We spoke to each other, there were words we could say to each other and to the evening, to the empty air, to the window beneath which we sat. From inside, music was pouring out into the courtyard, and the mountain looming over us looked darker than I had ever remembered it. The words, involuntarily, were themselves mere doubt, stipulations, promises. And these words that we pronounced to each other behind the house, in the darkness of the mountain, were followed by yet more words, there were letters traversing long routes, because the boy was studying engineering in Kharkov. Of his siblings he was the smallest, the lucky one. When he came home, he would have a diploma from the Soviet Union in his pocket; doors would open for him. He would know the slogans, at long last someone in the family could get somewhere.

And what business did I have there? What business would I have next to him? For the time being only to read about Kharkov. With its one million inhabitants, it was the second largest city in Ukraine, a significant industrial center:

among its many factories the largest one was the Malyshev Plant, where, under the direction of Mikhail Ilyich Koshkin, T-34 tanks were produced. The Soviet tanks thundered along in Kursk; they rumbled along in Debrecen, and they rumbled along to the south of Berlin, never even switching off their motors, they rumbled by Záhony, and then all along Bajczy-Zsilinszky Street. This is what one had to forget. Generally speaking, it isn't difficult to forget. To erase something, to chase it out of your head is easy, it's like knocking the kernel of the walnut out of its shell: you break the shell, you strike it against your palm, and the brown kernel falls out. You have to forget in such a way that nothing else remains, only the empty shell, from which—whoosh—a clever little squirrel has stolen the memories. It's better this way for you. My mother opposed the marriage, although she did not tell me why. Only later, much later, did she tell me, whispering in undertones, as if it would have meant something, that my husband's father was one of the men who left my grandfather behind on the snow-covered fields of Galicia. Do all stories end up circling round like this—do all crimes try to become something more subdued? Or, to the contrary, do they emerge when no one wants to remember them anymore, their heads suddenly popping up from beneath the snow? Run away, little squirrel, flee into your lair, I thought, let the foliage cover you, I will be grateful to you because you liberate me. From now on there will be no more yesterday, and there will be no more tomorrow. From now on, eternally there will only be today, an infinite day that will never pass, a day in which the youngest, luckiest son comes home, a laid table awaits him in the kitchen, and he tells stories and tells stories, and as a reward he will become chief engineer in a cement factory. The cement dust rises as if it were being sifted from beyond oblivion, it alights on every object thickly, and it is only the names that remain, nothing else, and my only task is to finish my courses at the university night school, to sit the state examination, to give birth to children, and to forget, to forget, all the while teaching history and literature in a school. A syllabus for our times, I say, and I begin to slide in present time, which is left empty: the age of primitive communities, the age of feudalism, the age of the republic, I say these words again and again, and I see the children's faces from somewhere far away, I see them and I keep sliding, as if I were sliding across a funnel imperceptibly, if not entirely unsuspectingly, for in the end I am sliding, without resistance, toward something that is unknown, unfathomable, and dark, and all the while I'm thinking of nothing but those luminous heights, thinking of that tiny city, of that square in that city where the young ladies show off their theatrical costumes in the windows and on the balconies, and mature women as well, some of them in pairs, others chatting in threes or fours, one window shares its news with another as they immerse themselves in the intricate life of the small city, in the never-ending discussions of business, family, but especially of romantic affairs. There, beneath the painted sky, which in the end is still more real than any other possible sky, is a place for every life; there every life finds a refuge. And now, in this moment, when I see myself on the verge of becoming lost, there, in the middle of the square stands a postman, his bag nearly bursting with letters, he looks up to the windows, but what is written upon his face, what can be read from it, I cannot see—

only those who are standing in the windows and on the balconies can see it.

What happened during these years that somehow would
not pass is not worthy of mention. It was a passing without movement, an enumeration of ruin in the midst of ep-
ochs slipping asunder—but no matter what it was, it is now
time for me to raise it up, to dispose of it, with good cheer,
and without somberness. It is time for me to dispose of the
face that was never completely my own, just as it was no one
else's; and yet I call it my face. Poor Johann Klarfeld never
could have known what enchanted him so fatally in Carlita's
empty gaze, just as he never could have known why Signor
del Filato had drawn him into the picture, and why he could
have belonged to that scene, so delicately suggestive, of Carlita's death. Well, it was because Carlita's face was almost
the perfect likeness of my own, just as two sand dunes or
two ocean waves are the near perfect likeness of each other.
If I were to say that Johann Klarfeld had fallen in love with
his own self contained in the likeness of an unattainable
woman, I would not be stating, but approaching, the truth,
inasmuch as is possible. He did not see me, he saw Carlita,
but Carlita's blindness was a mirror for him, just as his face is
a mirror for me, as are his eyes: the eyes of Johann Klarfeld,
which I now extinguish, I now make blind forever. For close
at hand is the quill of biography, that clavier faithful to every
human life, and all that remains to me now is to use it. "I, Johann Klarfeld—once upon a time, I was he—was born as a favored child of the stars on Wednesday, October 13, 1723, in
Bittenfeld, next to the town of Waiblingen, precisely at midday, as the church bells began to ring twelve." I shall run this

last course as well, and with this my service will be complete. The wanderings and fleeings of others have destined me to wander and flee as well, but I persevered, I remained, even if within nothingness, I spoke and I saw, if nothing else, then at least I saw two faces which I then placed together, because they belong together, although it is precisely two faces that belong together that cannot be joined. And already this is enough reason for me to say that in all times I have been, I am of good cheer. For nothing ever comes to an end, neither does it cease, it only disappears. Just as the snow ceases to fall, just as a snowflake melts away.

Closing Addresses

1

I have spoken, and you, my dear reader, have observed; and if you have paid attention well, perhaps you have discerned more than I wished to show. For he who writes shall be the lover of the evening, like a thief, whether he wishes it or not; and he shall see as many truths as there are grains of sand on the ocean's shore. But he who reads will be governed by the sun which illuminates everywhere; one must only wait for its time to come. And so for the reader time is always plentiful, there is no need to reach in haste for the doorknob and ask what the truth is. In daytime the thief rests, no need to fear him—and now as this book reaches its end, may the sun always shine upon its final pages, covering you, my dear reader, with glory, and myself with shame. For, having chosen the ink bottle of the writers of old, you see that I have become an author, although you may rest assured of my scorn for those who believe their humanity is dependent upon reaching an accord with the world as to their authorship. So now that ignominy has befallen me, as well. And I can hardly lull myself with the thought that my own authorship springs from the art of self-entrenchment, which—if one must write—is the single mode of the deliverance of souls, even should the body suffer from hunger, should it finally perish in the bleakest of fortifications. Never did I make arrangements for rescue; you will find me in the words, I who was the early pampered being of existence, I who became, amid the ages sliding asunder, the Angel of Ruin. And what can I say to you now, by way of farewell? Remain here, standing on the shore—do not follow in my footsteps!

2

It is neither my task nor yours to nourish ourselves with decay and plunge the earth into shadow; neither is it the task of life to emerge from seeds. Souls are not fertilized by blood and pain. Seek the path of gaiety, only that of gaiety—everywhere, gaiety!

Translator's Notes

The Rabbi Jeremiah ben Elazar said: This epigraph makes reference to the Talmud, Berakhot 61a. I have paraphrased the William Davidson translation at https://www.sefaria.org/Berakhot.61a.5?lang=bi, used under a Creative Commons license. The Talmud passage is itself a commentary on Psalm 139:5 (KJV): "Thou hast beset me behind and before, and laid thine hand upon me."

1. FLEEINGS

Gott, warum verstößest du uns für immer und bist so zornig über die Schafe deiner Weide?: A reference to Psalm 74:1: "O God, why hast thou cast us off for ever? Why doth thine anger smoke against the sheep of thy pasture?" (KJV).

Big Bertha: The short naval cannon, popularly known by the nickname Big Bertha, was a German siege howitzer used by the Imperial German Army from 1914 to 1918.

2. WITH WEARY EYES, BLINKING

When the Czechoslovak army marched into northern Hungary: The Hungarian-Czechoslovak War was fought between the short-lived Hungarian Soviet Republic and the army of the First Czechoslovak Republic from April to June 1919.

The Czechoslovaks soon left, and in their place came the Romanians: The Hungarian-Romanian War was fought between the Hungarian Soviet Republic and the Kingdom of Romania. Hostilities began in November

1918 and ended in August 1919. The Romanian army occupied eastern Hungary until March 28, 1920: this signified the defeat of the short-lived Communist rule in Hungary, after which Regent Miklós Horthy ascended to power.

He did not wish to switch allegiance and sign up with the Communist Party: Hungary was under Communist rule from 1948 to 1989.

After being sent to both Újvidék and Ruthenia: Újvidék is the Hungarian term for Novi Sad in today's Serbia; Carpathian Ruthenia was a region in the easternmost part of Czechoslovakia that became autonomous within that country in September 1938. It was occupied and annexed by Hungary in 1939, invaded by the Red Army in 1944, and incorporated into the Ukrainian Soviet Socialist Republic in 1946.

On the banks of the Dnieper: The Battle of the Dnieper took place in 1943 on the Eastern Front of World War II.

The regent himself, Miklós Horthy de Nagybánya: Miklós Horthy (1868–1957) assumed power in Hungary in 1920; in 1919, with the help of the Romanians and the French, he defeated the Communist government of Béla Kun. In 1944, he was deposed by Nazi Germany, with whom he had formed an alliance in 1939. Horthy oversaw the 1941 deportation of Hungarian Jews to Kamenetz-Podolsk (a subject treated in Schein's novel *Lazarus* [trans. Ottilie Mulzet; London: Seagull Books, 2017]), pogroms against Hungarian Jews and Serbs in Újvidék, and the 1944 deportations of nearly five hundred thousand Hungarian Jews to the death camps of the Third Reich, as well as twenty-eight thousand Roma.

Virgins' Baths: Today the site of the Gellért Hotel and Baths.

Here on the banks of the Danube: This passage quotes the words spoken by Horthy in his speech on November 16, 1919, given in Budapest.

He did not approve of this great mutual embrace of Jew and Hungarian: The second half of the nineteenth century represented a period of rapid assimilation for the Jews of Hungary.

3. THINGS NEAR AND FAR AWAY

When the Tatars, with their shrieking yelps, attacked the village from the south: A reference to Mongolian incursions into the Carpathian basin in the mid- to late thirteenth century.

The siege of Eger in 1552: This took place during the Ottoman wars of the sixteenth century; Hungary was under Ottoman rule from 1541 to 1699.

Géza Gárdonyi's novel Eclipse of the Crescent Moon: First published in 1899, *Eclipse of the Crescent Moon (Egri csillagok)* tells the story of the occupation of Buda and the siege of Eger by the Ottoman Empire; it is based on historical events but includes fictional characters. It was translated into English by George Cushing.

The Beg of Fülek: Beg (or Bey) was an Ottoman title, based on an older Turkic term for chieftain. Fülek is the town of Fil'akovo in today's Slovakia.

After the death of the last of the Bárius family: The Bárius family was granted land in Borsod County in Hungary by Sigismund of Luxembourg as a reward for having taken part in the Crusades in the late fourteenth century.

The noble Vays: A noble family in Hungary originating in the early thirteenth century.

Rákóczi's uprising: Ferenc Rákóczi (1676–1735) was a Hungarian nobleman who led the uprising against the Habsburgs in 1703–1711.

When the French and the Austrians, battling each other in the Rhineland, finally sat down to talks in Vienna: This refers to the Aachen 1748 peace treaty following the War of the Austrian Succession.

As Heinrich Heine believed: The German poet Heinrich Heine (1797–1856) wrote a poem celebrating cholent.

The Third Anti-Jewish Law of August 1941: Hungary's Third Anti-Jewish Law, which was similar to the Nazi Nuremberg Laws, was put into effect in 1941.

Balázs Ományi fell at Mohács yesterday: Balázs Ományi fought in the Battle of Mohács in 1526 (when central Hungary fell to the Ottomans).

If you own at least ten holds *of land, I'll take you:* A Hungarian *hold* is an old land measurement (*hold,* "moon," from Latin *juger* or *jugerum,* the area of land plowed before the moon rose). There are various subcategories; here it refers to a "little hold," approximately 3.5 square meters.

But he nearly perished at the Dnieper: A reference to Operation Barabossa in World War II, when poorly equipped Hungarian soldiers were obliged to fight against the Soviet Union.

4. A PRESENT FOR FATHER DOLPHUS

Just as Jesus cast out the demons in the form of pigs from the demon-possessed: A reference to and paraphrase of Matthew 8:28–34, Mark 5:1–20, and Luke 8:26–39. In the original biblical parable, the demons ask Jesus to be cast out in the form of swine, and he consents.

It was published by Jacobus Zegers in Leuven in 1640: Jacobus Zegers (d. 1644) was an academic printer and bookseller in Leuven. Among other titles, he printed Cornelius Jansen's massive three-volume *Augustinus* in 1640, which was subsequently condemned by the pope.

He trampled down the head of Pelagius: Pelagius (c. 354–418) was a theologian who advocated free will and asceticism. Augustine of Hippo accused him of denying the need for divine aid in performing good works. Pelagius refuted Augustine's theory of original sin. He was declared a heretic by the Council of Ephesus in 431 and expelled from Jerusalem, but allowed to settle in Egypt.

My surgeon master: Barbers in the eighteenth century and previously often performed minor surgical procedures; they were also known, in a military context, as feldshers.

The Etymologicum magnum: *Etymologicum Magnum* is a Greek lexical encyclopedia compiled at Constantinople by an unknown lexicographer around 1150 CE. It is the largest Byzantine lexicon and draws on many earlier grammatical, lexical, and rhetorical works.

5. IN THE GARB OF BABEL

He had no need for a feldsher: The term *feldsher* was used for barber surgeons in the German and Swiss armies from the seventeenth century until professional military medical services were established, first by Prussia in the early eighteenth century. Barbers performed amputations, applied leeches, and did other surgeries.

The Kalnocky Hussars: The Kalnocky Hussars were regiments sent by Hungary to fight in the War of the Austrian Secession. Colonel Anton Count Kálnoky was commander of the regiment. (Kalnocky is the German spelling of Kálnoky.)

Baron Munchausen: Baron Munchausen is a fictional German nobleman created by the German writer Rudolf Erich Raspe (1736–1794) in his 1785 book *Baron Munchausen's Narrative of His Marvelous Travels and Campaigns in Russia.* The character is loosely based on a real baron, Hieronymus Karl Friedrich, Freiherr von Münchhausen.

6. THE REPORT OF A PISTOL

Mátyás Rákosi: Mátyás Rákosi (1892–1971) was the leader of Hungary's Communist Party from 1945 to 1956; from 1949 to 1956 he was the ruler of Communist Hungary.

Kannst du es begreifen . . . du kannst weg, bleibst jedoch hier, denn alles geschieht gleichzeitig: "Can you understand . . . you can leave and yet you remain here, because everything happens simultaneously."

An agent of the State Protection Authority: The Hungarian State Protection Authority (Államvédelmi Hatóság) was the secret police of the Hungarian Communist state from 1948 to 1956.

Three wise men with three sorrowful gazes: Marx, Engels, and Lenin.

German Parabellum: A type of German pistol, manufactured from the late nineteenth century until 1948.

Two alternating state powers: A reference to Hungary when it was an ally of Nazi Germany (1939–1945) and then Communist Hungary (1948–1989).

Sándor Petőfi, Mihály Vörösmarty, and János Arany: Sándor Petőfi (1823–1849) was a Hungarian revolutionary poet; Mihály Vörösmarty (1800–1855) was a dramatist and poet, one of the great figures of the Hungarian Romantic era; and János Arany (1812–1882) was a poet, writer, and translator, as well as a famous composer of ballads.

For he was the one who said to hang all the kings: A reference to a famous poem of Petőfi's, "Hang All the Kings!" ("Akasszátok föl a királyokat!").

Close your eyes, he said, if you don't believe, if you don't believe that it is I; and ask your heart, for surely that shall give reply: A paraphrase from Petőfi's famous poem "With Mihály Tompa" ("Tompa Mihálynál"). Mihály Tompa (1819–1868) was a lyric poet and Calvinist minister.

For surely of an evening, sorrowful Petőfi he did see, indeed by day as well: A paraphrase from János Arany's poem, "Memories" ("Emlények").

No specter of troubles for which we must atone?: A paraphrase from Mihály Vörösmarty's poem "What Shall We Do?" ("Mit csinálunk?").

"If he disobeys the law, he'll get stuck on a branch, he will pay in this world and in the next!": A quotation from János Arany's epic poetic trilogy based on the life of Miklós Toldi, a fourteenth-century Hungarian culture hero.

For mourning and blood shall be the fate of the Hungarian people: A quotation from Sándor Petőfi, the refrain to "A Song of Black and Red" ("Fekete-piros dal").

God has ordered poets so to lead!: This is a paraphrase of a fragment from Petőfi, from *The Poets of the Nineteenth Century (A XIX. század költői)*. Edwin Morgan's translation in part reads:

God had sent to guide his flock.
In our days God has ordered poets
to be the fiery pillars and
so to lead the wandering people
into Canaan's promised land.

Shako: A tall, cylindrical military cap, usually with a visor, and sometimes tapered at the top.

"Summons": The "Summons" ("Szózat") was written in 1836 by Mihály Vörösmarty, set to music, and first performed on May 10, 1843, in the National Theater. There was a debate about whether "Summons" or Ferenc Kölcsey's "Hymn" ("Himnusz") should be chosen as the Hungarian national anthem.

Next to the house of the steward, in a smaller house, was born the poet who was named as the chief of all Hungarian poets: A reference to Count József Gvadányi (1725–1801), general and writer.

Ferenc Kazinczy: Ferenc Kazinczy (1759–1831) was a Hungarian author, poet, translator, and one of the most important figures in the movement of the renewal of the Hungarian language and literature at the turn of the nineteenth century.

Pál Rontó: Pál Rontó (Rontó Pál, 1793) is an epic verse narration written by József Gvadányi. It tells the story of Pál Rontó ("Pál the Spoiler"), a clever peasant boy who becomes a hussar and eventually has to escape to Poland.

Gypsy bread: Bread baked from dough remnants.

The last Hungarian revolution: The Hungarian Revolution of 1956.

There was no knife yet in the heart of Lamberg, no noose around the neck of Latour: A paraphrase from Petőfi's "Hang All the Kings!," it references two figures, Count Franz Philipp von Lamberg (1791–1848), an Austrian soldier and statesman who was killed by a mob during the Hungarian Revolution of 1848 (after which the Imperial Court in Vienna decided to dissolve the Hungarian Parliament and send Serbian troops into Hungary); and Theodor Franz, Count of Baillet von Latour (1780–1848), an Austrian soldier and statesman who, as imperial minister of war, was killed by a mob at the beginning of the Vienna Uprising.

Imre Gáti: On October 26, 1956, in Miskolc, Lajos Freimann and Gyula Gáti, Imre Gáti's cousin, were both lynched. Antal Bokor is a fictional character.

In the summer of 1946, a mob had lynched some black marketeers because they thought they were Jewish: This attack is known as the Miskolc Pogrom.

GAZ-M20 Pobeda: The GAZ-M20 Pobeda was a passenger car produced in the Soviet Union by GAZ from 1946 until 1958.

Four Russians riding in an open UAZ military vehicle: Abbreviation of *Ulyanovsky Avtomobilny Zavod* (Ulyanovsk Automobile Plant), known for the UAZ-469, a light utility vehicle.

Seder: "Order, arrangement" in Hebrew.

The man interpreting said, "Paryadok. On sledil za paryadokom": Russian for "Order. He kept order."

Kak tu skazesh pa vengerskij "paryadok"? Nikak, nikak: Russian for "How do you say 'order' in Hungarian? Not at all, not at all."

7. SECRET THEATER

Lajos Batthyány: Count Lajos Batthyány de Németújvár (1807–1849) was the first prime minister of Hungary, appointed during the revolution of 1848. On the order of the Austrian Empire, he was executed by firing squad in Pest on October 6, 1849, the same day as the 13 Martyrs of Arad (who also rebelled against Austria).

8. THE MOUTHS OF THE SACKS ARE LOOSENED

Babel Babel abba bolal Babel Babel abba bolal kol kol kol: A ditty of Hebrew words, which translates as "Babel Babel papa muddle Babel Babel papa muddle all all all." These are references to Genesis 11:7–9 (KJV): "Go to, let us go down, and there confound their language, that they may not understand one another's speech. So the Lord scattered them abroad from thence upon the face of all the earth: and they left off to build the city. Therefore is the name of it called Babel; because the Lord did there confound the language of all the earth: and from thence did the Lord scatter them abroad upon the face of all the earth."

9. CONCEALED MAP

John Maurice, prince of Nassau-Siegen: John Maurice (1604–1679) was the builder of the Mauritshuis; he was also the governor of Dutch Brazil.

10. THE BEAUTIFUL HARMONIES OF RUIN

We were something like Ági Balázs in Rainy Sunday: *Rainy Sunday* (dir. Mar-tón Keleti, 1962) tells the story of a group of girls in a Budapest high school. They are all taken with the handsome new teacher, Pali, who falls in love with the "star student" Ági. Ági is frightened by his approaches, however, so he finds consolation in the arms of the class bombshell, Olga Bakonyi.

    Poor dear old Alfred Krupp: Alfred Krupp (1812–1887) was a German industrialist known for the development and worldwide sale of cast-steel cannons. Under his direction, the Krupp Works began manufacturing ordnance in the 1840s.

    Hungarian Communist Youth Organization: The Hungarian Communist Youth Organization (Magyar Kommunista Ifjúsági Szövetség) was founded after the 1956 revolution, with the ostensible purpose of educating youth. It was in operation until 1989.

    Attila József: Attila József (1905–1937), one of the most beloved Hungarian poets of the twentieth century, came from a working-class background and during the Communist era was hailed as a great poet of proletarian origins.

GÁBOR SCHEIN is the author of ten books of prose and five books of poetry. His work has been translated into French, German, and Spanish, among other languages. He is a writer of fierce moral and aesthetic independence whose subjects include trauma and survivorhood in central Europe and post-regime change Budapest. His novellas *The Book of Mordechai* (translated by Adam Z. Levy) and *Lazarus* (translated by Ottilie Mulzet) were published in one volume by Seagull Books.

OTTILIE MULZET was awarded the National Book Award for Translated Literature in 2019 for her translation of *Baron Wenckheim's Homecoming* by László Krasznahorkai. She has also translated the work of Szilárd Borbély, György Dragomán, and László Földényi, the last-mentioned author for Yale University Press.

Ottilie Mulzet would like to thank the Hungarian Translators' House in Balatonfüred, Hungary, where this translation was partially completed, for their kind support.